To Eva,

CaraMarie Christy

I wrote this book when I was very little. Sometimes my fairies can be scary, so let Grandma know when to skip the scary parts. This book shows you can do a lot, even when you're young, if you read lots and study hard! Good luck on your Chinese and I hope you enjoy my fairies.

OAKTARA

WATERFORD, VIRGINIA

CaraMarie Christy

Fairies Fly

Published in the U.S. by:
OakTara Publishers
P.O. Box 8
Waterford, VA 20197

Visit OakTara at
www.oaktara.com

Cover design by Muses9 Design
Cover image fairy© iStockphoto.com/Casarsa
Cover image wings: iStockphoto.com/sx70

Copyright © 2009 by CaraMarie Christy. All rights reserved.

ISBN: 978-1-60290-215-2

Fairies Fly is a work of fiction. References to real people, events, establishments, organizations, or locales are intended only to provide a sense of authenticity and are used fictitiously. All other characters, incidents, and dialogue are drawn from the author's imagination.

To everyone
who has made me laugh, smile, cry,
(or do all of those at once)
because, chances are,
you've inspired
at least one character in my stories.

Acknowledgments

Thanks to:

My friends for putting up with my excitement through the process;

My family members for their love and encouragement;

OakTara, for publishing this novel.

One

Kendra ran through the rain with childish joy. She remembered doing things like this when she was younger, only it hadn't been nearly as wet...and she or one of her friends would have been playing the part of the bad guy.

But the person stalking sixteen-year-old Kendra and her friend, Maddy, was no friend wanting to play, and the gun he was holding under his black overcoat was not a plastic child's toy.

Pushing through the umbrella-equipped New York crowd, heading home to their apartments after a hard day of work, Kendra glanced back. Maddy was struggling, his height and broad shoulders making it harder to move quickly through the mass of bodies. He had slowed to a steady walk, while Kendra moved like a minnow in a river, swift and uncatchable.

Dodging a sharp-tipped purple umbrella, Kendra backtracked to grab Maddy's arm and pulled him forward. "Faster, Maddy."

People had said Kendra's voice had the slight musical tone that made it seem almost inhuman. *Oh, how very right those people are*, she thought.

Maddy trudged on, trying his best to quicken his pace. He wasn't used to it—the pounding fear and the dread of possibly having a gun pointed in his face.

Kendra, on the other hand, loved the rush of it all. It was what her kind lived for. Fairies couldn't get enough of adrenaline rushes. Their human forms even loved the rush of fear mixed with that strange, alluring excitement.

The human form of Kendra was—no denying it—pretty. Velvet blue eyes shone from her heart-shaped face, framed by waves of flame-colored hair. A button nose and rose red lips gave the slightest hint as to what she really was. Her body was that of someone who worked hard to stay in shape; in years to come, she knew it would pay off. She wore a slightly faded pair of boot cut jeans and a blue *Save the whales* T-shirt.

Ten yards ahead Kendra saw a back alley—a place where even people in a group feared to tread.

"Maddy," she whispered, "let's turn off there," and she pointed so the man forcing himself through the crowd five yards behind them wouldn't be able to hear. Not that he'd have been able to hear them anyway since the crowd surrounding them was making a thunderous racket.

"Oh, so instead of getting shot by a strange man, we're going to be beaten to death by thugs," Maddy joked. He shot Kendra a weak, forced grin.

"Shut up and move," she said, her voice now urgent because she feared for Maddy's life.

She didn't even think about her own, since it's impossible for fairies to fear for their own lives, even the Dark Fairies, who are as selfish as one could possibly be. Somewhere along their ancestry line fairies had lost their ability to fear for their own well-being. But they loved their families and friends.

As soon as they reached the alley, Kendra pulled a slightly unwilling Maddy about ten steps into the darkness, then pushed him and herself flat against the brick wall of a building.

Some fairies have a hard time using their magic, but for Kendra, using her powers came as easily as breathing. One minute two teenagers were holding hands and pressing themselves frantically against the wall...and the next there was only the red brick wall.

But they were too late. Just as Kendra used her powers, the

menacing, large man reached the alley. With a couple quick steps he grabbed Kendra, where she stood, invisible, and pointed a gun to her forehead.

Letting the magic slip away, Kendra allowed herself to become visible again. She bowed her head, hoping to die a painless death.

Boom!

Kendra's last thoughts were of Maddy.

೯ം‍ം‍ട

The sun was shining through white hospital curtains when Kendra awoke. A quick peek in the nearby mirror revealed that her long copper hair was in desperate need of a good brushing, so she pulled at it with her fingers. Her blue eyes looked tired, defeated. Somehow she had fallen asleep in the uncomfortable, red plastic guest chair.

Stretching and yawning, she paced about the room, remembering what had happened the night before and why her young friend was lying on the bed in front of her with bandages wrapped around his shoulder....

೯ം‍ം‍ട

Maddy stood, invisible, watching the thug grab Kendra. But as soon as the man put the gun to Kendra's head, Maddy took action. Jumping on top of the giant thug, Maddy forced him down and away from Kendra. But the man's gunshot went wild and lodged in Maddy's shoulder.

Kendra stood, paralyzed by fright, as her friend willingly threw his life in danger to protect her. Then he crumpled to the ground with a cry of agony.

Seconds later, as the thug struggled to get to his feet, two NY policemen entered the alleyway, guns drawn. They'd pinned the man up against a wall and handcuffed him, then called for an ambulance.

The paramedics in the red and white vehicle with the blaring siren and flashing lights had checked Kendra and Maddy over quickly, then loaded Maddy onto a stretcher. Kendra stood, terrified by the sight of her injured friend, next to him, holding his hand.

She had known Maddy her whole life. But now his green eyes—usually so full of mystery and fun—stared blankly at the white ceiling of the ambulance. His short black hair, usually curly at the tips, lay flat against his head, glued there by sweat. His muscled body—he was a head taller than Kendra and could pick her up with ease—lay still. Numerous medical instruments swayed eerily around the stretcher as though he were a corpse from a horror movie.

The ride to the hospital passed in a blur. The paramedics attempted to engage her in some friendly small talk, but Kendra remained quiet, politely nodding only where it seemed fit to do so. While the paramedics were around she dared not use magic to heal her friend's wound. It would have risked revealing all she held dear to the fairy hunters....

❦

Humans who learn of the fairy secret from the passing of information throughout history always pass it on to their children. Some see it as just a silly superstition; others take up the tradition of hunting the fairies down.

You see, fairies are known for three things: the magical healing properties of their blood; the tough, bullet-proof material their wings are made of; and the magical properties stored inside their silver tears. The only way to kill a fairy is by inserting something made of lead inside her brain (which is why fairies are deathly afraid of guns), waiting two hundred years for her to die of old age, or to force her to bleed to death, which is the hardest possibility by far, seeing as fairies have healing abilities that far surpass anything any doctor could do.

Back at the hospital Kendra had watched as the medical team worked on Maddy in ER, then moved him to his own private room. They had allowed her to stay through the night. As they came in and out of the room, Kendra had waited for the opportunity to put her healing powers to use…but had fallen asleep.

Now, in the bright light of morning, she set to work magically healing Maddy's wound. It wasn't an easy task, for every now and then she had to stop and hurriedly rewrap the bandages on his shoulder before a doctor came by. The bullet had gone deep, almost all the way through his shoulder, and had torn a lot of tissue.

Kendra finished her handiwork. She smiled, satisfied. Not even a scar remained.

"Thanks," a voice said.

Kendra jumped. Maddy's eyes fluttered open and he grinned wickedly. The eyes Kendra loved so much were back to normal now, glinting with mischief. He reached over and rubbed the place where the hole in his shoulder had been.

"It should itch, but that usually goes away after awhile." Kendra knew her facts well, for Maddy had indeed been about to scratch at his shoulder. "You saved my life," Kendra said quietly.

"Don't mention it," Maddy replied with another grin.

They sat in silence for a few moments. Kendra wondered what Maddy was thinking.

Bang!

The door to the hospital room flung open and crashed into a nearby wall. Kendra's mom made such a grand entrance that Kendra shook her head and stared down at the floor in embarrassment.

Myna was, you could say, quite odd. Her rainbow-colored robe, which she always wore in public, made her stand out in a crowd. Her hair was the same flame color as her daughter's, but her eyes were emerald green. She also had a rounder, more jubilant face, covered in the most outrageous neon makeup to match her robe. Beads of all sorts hung about her neck, while her earlobes looked as if they were being pulled down to the ground by a jumbled assortment of hoop earrings.

No one would ever have realized this crazy woman was a very powerful and beautiful fairy in her true form. That was the most important reason Myna wore the costume, besides the fact she was quite dramatic and loved to make grand appearances wherever she went. People just thought she was a loony old bat, not a threat to anyone, except maybe herself. But when alone with her daughter, Myna would take off the costume, revealing her beautiful fairy form underneath.

Maddy had never seen Myna's true form, though she had assured him it was quite spectacular, so he was used to the way Myna's human form looked and enjoyed seeing the woman who was ten times more bizarre then his own parents.

"Seems you've been magically healed. Looks like doctors can work miracles these days." Myna gave a knowing glance at Kendra, who grinned in response. The air of command in Myna's voice that was very much like Kendra's. "You should be grateful that you're alive."

So the long speech, of the danger had anyone seen them disappearing from the fairy hunter, was about to be heard for the millionth time. But, strangely, that speech did not come. Instead Myna just seemed to lose her trail of thought and stared off into space for a couple of minutes.

That, for some odd reason, made Kendra feel extremely guilty. Once she'd spotted the man she knew was a fairy hunter, the adrenaline of the chase had surged within her. She'd lost control and made a run for it. A normal person wouldn't have done that, so that loss of control had flagged for the fairy hunter just who she and Maddy were.

It was amazing how such a simple thing as a walk to the grocery store could turn into a trip to the hospital.

Two doctors wearing their green gown-like uniforms walked in. They seemed flabbergasted at not only the strange woman sitting in the room, though that may have been a big part of it, but also how it was possible for a young man who had just had a bullet in his shoulder to have healed so quickly.

Unable to give an explanation, the befuddled doctors gave back Maddy's clothes, for he had been wearing a hospital gown, and released him from the facility.

In the fresh air of the parking lot it was hard to have imagined Maddy in the stretcher looking horrible, Kendra thought, as he flashed a smile at her and grabbed her left hand. He seemed full of energy and life, unlike when he was in the ambulance when he could have passed for a dead person.

☙❧

Myna ignored the two kids following her, not liking the fact that her own daughter was getting too close to a human. Kendra had always been stubborn, even when she was a young child. No one was ever going to be able to force Kendra to do something she didn't want to do. So when she turned fifteen, the age many young fairies would have been married, she had told her mother she would marry when she was ready. Being a reasonable mother Myna had let her daughter make one of the biggest decisions of her life on her own.

Parked in practically the dead center of all the cars was a van. You could tell it was Myna's from the fact that it stood out from the other vehicles around it. Neon peace signs covered every free space on the car except for the windows. Inside, purple fake fur covered the floor, seats, and even the steering wheel while the rest of the inside matched with purple paint.

Maddy chuckled as he sat down in one of the back seats, while Kendra rode shotgun. Myna turned on the ignition and the car roared to life. She was a fairly decent driver, if not a little wide on her turns, and, for practically the first time, she got them back to her house without any problems.

Unlike the rest of the items Myna owned, the house she and Kendra lived in looked quite normal—at least to most people from the outside. It was a large condo, slightly surrounded by trees for some privacy from the two large condos on either side. There was a small piece of land covered in gravel that served as a driveway, which Myna pulled into.

Inside the house was another story. An odd assortment of herbs and powders were stacked in every free space available. Once, when they were kids, Maddy had been afraid that he might find a disembodied organ of an animal, but Kendra had assured him that they only ever used plants in their spells. Books also littered the house, some with markers sticking out of them to keep the place of a certain important spell or potion.

"Man, my dad's condo looks so normal compared to this place," Maddy said enviously, like he couldn't get enough of the weird stuff that surrounded Kendra and her mother.

You're probably wondering how a small cottage between two condos managed to go unnoticed as a possible fairy hideout. It had taken Myna a short time to make a potion called Hiding Heather, which rendered a house or piece of land to look exactly like its surroundings. Kendra (even though she was only five years old at the time) and Myna had stood on the roof in the middle of the night to drop a pan full of the potion to make the house look like just another condo. To those who knew the cottage was there and had seen it before the potion was dumped on, it still looked like its original self—a rundown condo that nobody seemed to live in.

Kendra began making a simple potion in one of the slightly

dirty pans sitting on a desk that served as her very own workspace. After five seconds of staring at the ingredients, she asked Maddy to go out in the back garden and get her certain herbs and berries. He did as she asked and went out a small green door, Myna following him to get ingredients of her own.

Five minutes later there were loud shouts, one of them easily recognized as Maddy's deep voice, and bangs from the garden.

Kendra rushed outside to the small forest-like garden of strange plants and herbs. Pushing her way through a tall crop of yellow berries and fighting off a plant that was determined to grab her ankle, she found her mother lying on the ground and Maddy nowhere in the small clearing.

Two

She was beautiful, unlike many of the dark rulers who came before her. But nobody really noticed this when they were being tortured and threatened mercilessly for information concerning the three other rulers.

The Dark Queen had no problem threatening information out of innocent victims. She had lost her heart when a boy she loved dearly disappeared. Afterwards she married the Dark King, who had been asking for her hand in marriage for years, then killed him in his sleep rather than spending the rest of her life with the despicable and terribly ugly old man.

The queen of Air, queen of Light, and king of Earth all disapproved of the queen's ways to rule a country, but they were near powerless to stop her.

"Corner, get over here—" the female voice was cold and cruel—"go to dungeon A to see if one of our Air Fairy prisoners are talking."

Looking only slightly older than she had ten years ago when she lost her heart, Kendra's hair was still flame red, but her blue eyes had become cold, icy, and lifeless.

Corner, her young dark-haired, dark-eyed assistant, ran into the room. He resembled a mouse while Kendra resembled a fox and it looked like she easily could have gobbled him up if she wanted to. Once again he came back with unpleasing news, gaining him a nasty, terrifying look.

Nobody in dungeon A had ever confessed any important information. Air Fairies were a loyal bunch, and the queen remembered being one. It was pointless to continue torturing them, but she refused to give up.

"Hurt them on the inside. Make sure the beaters find out what is really painful for them. If possible, find their families and threaten to kill them. Also, make sure our SPECIAL guest doesn't see his daughter again...you remember the plan we talked about?"

Her assistant nodded in reply and ran off at once to give out the commands. A grim smile played across the beautiful queen's face; she knew the hurt of losing someone you loved dearly.

☙❧

As soon as the Dark Queen gained power, Jacob Andrews suddenly disappeared. His daughter, Cassandra, was left on her own, for only one parent is allowed to care for a child in the fairy world. Her next-door neighbors had helped her get settled with a job at a local food market, and in her spare time she continued searching for her missing father.

The letter that came to the thirteen-year-old was hardly a surprise. After reading it she had begun putting security spells on every space that might be big enough for someone to slip into, knowing she had to get into Earth King Territory in Canada as fast as possible.

Dark Fairy Territory stretched through all fifty states of America. If someone has ever disappeared where you live, well, I guess you know why now.

Cassandra knew the letter informing her that her dad had been taken in for questioning, and that to free him she would need to come to the Dark Queen's mansion, was a trap. But she had to do something. Putting the note on her neighbor's doorstep to explain why she was leaving, Cassandra headed north.

She was very beautiful, with the build of a young athlete.

A wild, golden blond mane reached nearly to her waist, and her eyes were a sea green, lightly blue around the edges. Slightly short for her age, Cassandra stood 4' 7", almost as tall as her favorite tree that stood in front of the house she was now leaving.

A pair of dark jean capris, a faded jean jacket, a disco flower belt with a matching band wrapped around her forehead, a chain necklace with a neon purple peace sign charm, and a neon orange T-shirt made Cassandra look like the cool hippie she was. The only uncool thing she was forced to wear were a small pair of green rectangular glasses.

To supply her with anything she needed from the house Cassandra dragged a black suitcase with her. She had poured a potion in it so that all she needed to do was say what she wanted clearly to the inside of the suitcase or think hard about the item in her mind's eye, and if it was in her house it would come to her. Putting the item back in the suitcase would return it back to its original position in the house.

Now Cassandra was jogging through a nearly deserted street. It was October in New York, so she gripped her jacket to keep the chill out of her bones. Freezing, howling wind whipped itself at her ears, and Cassandra felt they were going numb. Her feet were hitting the ground slower than they had been when she first started.

"Come on, I only ran one and a half miles," she mumbled to herself.

A man walking by gave her a weird look, for she seemed to be talking to her feet. She gave him a small smile just to show she had been kidding, and slowed her pace to a walk to conserve energy. Stores and some closed buildings not used for anything lined the sidewalk on her right, while the road and a few parked cars were on her left.

Grumble.

Her stomach was sore from lack of lunch, but she knew she

had to conserve her resources. Only halfway through New York, Cassandra had tried a few different buses to get farther north. Each had mysteriously run out of gas, which Cassandra was sure wasn't a coincidence.

Storm clouds had started brewing overhead, so she had to get into an enclosed room fast. Dark Fairies could track anyone they wanted if they were outside too long.

Walking into a nearby café, Cassandra ordered bottled water. She had been walking since morning—right after she'd eaten a small breakfast and read the letter from the Dark Fairy Queen.

The café she was resting in was quiet and calming, with a lot of round tables scattered about the place and the smell of coffee hanging thick in the air. It was the kind of place where you could almost fall asleep.

And that's exactly what Cassandra did....

Darkness surrounded her as she walked forward along a tunnel. At the end she could see a light and the silhouette of a tall man. Closer up, he looked like the older male version of Cassandra.

"Seems like you're on the run," said the rough voice she knew so well. "I guess that would be all my fault. Before time runs out, I must tell you something: the queen's heart is not completely lost to darkness. The cure for her was in the soul of a young man, a human man. Once the queen loved him dearly, but she assumed he had abandoned her and was a traitor who killed her mother. I'm talking to you through Air Fairy Dreams, you know that spell well, but now they are also able to locate you unless you're in an enclosed building."

The dream version of Cassandra just stared blankly at her father, taking in everything he said.

"Be careful, for the man you must seek for the freedom of everyone in the Dark Fairy Territory is surrounded by fairy hunters and fairies alike. One wrong move and you'll be killed.

That, or tell someone else about the man, someone you can trust. You're the only one I can relay this information to, which I found out through spies in the mansion, and I have faith that you'll find someone to complete or help you complete the quest.

"If the man you seek is dead, then do not fear that all is lost. Your soul will find the answer and lead you to someone who can tell you the truth. I'm probably the worst father in the world for not telling you the truth when you were ready to hear it. But all things play out certain ways for a reason."

As the two were walking, it began to get brighter and brighter, until finally it was so bright it burned Cassandra's eyes, and she woke up. Her head had been leaning on her hand and she was drooling slightly. After wiping her mouth on her jacket, she tipped her waitress, went to the restroom, and checked the skies outside.

It seemed to be clearing up, with only a few stray clouds now littering the heavens above. Cassandra cautiously walked outside and began jogging once again north. The fact that it may possibly be a race with somebody chasing her made her fairy blood boil slightly.

She didn't know what else to do. Never having gone to Canada, Cassandra only knew that her father had friends up there.

"Maybe I could talk to the king," Cassandra thought out loud. The next instant she knew it was a stupid idea. It was known that the queen once had a soul and that she had been an Air Fairy, just like Cassandra.

One thing was for certain, though. As both parts of Cassandra's common sense battled it out inside her head, the answer was up in Earth Fairy Territory.

A gray, aging bus stopped twenty feet in front of where Cassandra was standing and she ran to catch it. After asking the bus driver whether or not the bus was going north, she got on.

The seats were a little pathetic, with many wires sticking out of the green/purple colored bench, all of which she was careful to avoid. A man in the seat behind her was snoring loudly. Another man wearing a dark cloak that hid his features seemed to be watching her every move, so Cassandra was careful to calmly avoid him in case he was a fairy hunter.

When the aging bus stopped in front of an old train station, Cassandra and the man wearing the dark cloak both got off.

She bought a ticket to get her as far north to Canada as possible. When she was there she planned to get on a Middle Berg subway to a local train station that would, hopefully, get her to another train that would transport her right into Canada. It seemed a good plan, though she had no clue how close to the subway station the train would take her.

Then, all of a sudden, someone grabbed her arm hard and slammed her into the gray stone wall of the train station. Her suitcase was flung from her grasp and landed with a clatter on the hard cement floor.

Pale green eyes looked into her light, sea green ones.

Three

Madore could scent a fairy from a mile away, so when the little Air Fairy girl walked onto the bus, he had known her at once for what she really was...as though he were a fairy himself.

"Whatever you do, don't scream." He said it firmly, for the girl looked on the verge of yelling for help.

Just then an officer approached, eyes narrowed, at having seen a full-grown man throwing a thirteen-year-old girl up against a wall.

Having spent five years researching Air Fairies and how how to play this kind of part, Madore knew his next line. "You will not smoke cigarettes and that is final," he told her. Releasing his grip slightly on the girl, he stood back to see what she would do.

For an instant she looked confused, then she blurted, "Fine, but all my friends say it's cool."

Madore had to hand it to her. She was a good actress. He knew no fairy could smoke cigarettes.

The policeman frowned. "Next time, sir, I suggest not using as much force. I realize smoking is very bad, especially for teenagers, but it looked like you were hurting your child." Then he walked away.

☙❧

At first Cassandra thought the man was a fairy hunter. Then she reconsidered. If he was, then he'd be leading her to a back alley to kill her where nobody would see. He certainly wouldn't be engaging her in conversation.

"So where are we going, *Dad?*" Cassandra said the word with an air of distaste, knowing the man in front of her could never be her father. She bent to pick up her suitcase.

For the first time Cassandra was able to see the cloaked man's face. His features were dark, except for his bright emerald green eyes. Curly black hair lay unkempt and dirty, and he had the beginnings of a beard and mustache, which only helped to darken his features further. At one time he might have been handsome, but the world had not been kind to him, for he seemed terribly thin.

"*Daughter,* please call me by my full name, Madore," he replied sarcastically, "And I thought you wanted to go read at the new Smelter Library across the street."

Cassandra allowed the man to steer her out of the train station, throwing her ticket to a homeless man with a sign saying *Help Me Go North*. The man whooped and hollered with joy as she and Madore left through a large archway marked with a blinking exit sign.

The library was nice enough, with towering shelves reaching up to the domed ceiling. The musty smell of old books hung thick, and the silence was pressing. If a mouse had scampered by, it would have been heard clearly.

A small section in the back of the library was completely empty, with not even a librarian with thick-rimmed glasses waiting around a corner to catch unsuspecting, noisy teenagers. No, this section seemed untouched. The old leather-bound books appeared ancient for such a new library.

Cassandra pried a random book out of one of the shelves and was not surprised by what she saw. It was a book of mystical beings, fairies, goblins, and all other sorts of oddball creatures. Though some books would give you the little-kid version of what mystical beings were, others, if you looked in just the right spot, would tell you everything you needed to know.

The book Cassandra picked up was just such a book. Gold letters, which she recognized from the swirling words as Air Fairy script, stood out from the black leather cover. Pictures inside showed Air Fairies in their true forms and human forms, though the book didn't indicate who the people were.

Beautiful wasn't a word to describe fairies in their natural form. They couldn't be described by mere words. For Air Fairies, flowing, moon silver hair fell down past their waists, while two pairs of white translucent wings, all four embedded with the jeweled swirl symbol of the Air Fairies, sparkled as if moonlight was always hitting them. Silver eyes didn't make the fairies look weird; they just made them look more amazing. Each wore a robe of light blue, with dark blue swirl symbols, the same ones that were on their wings, covering most of the robe.

Cassandra was used to the sight of people like her. Having grown up in her fairy form to make sure by the time she was older that her magic would be able to sustain a solid human form, or she would have risked being seen for what she was, she had looked in a mirror to admire her reflection more than once.

Four oak wood chairs were scattered in the corner, where there were no book shelves.

"What type of fairy are you?" the man asked bluntly.

"I have no clue what you're talking about," Cassandra said convincingly.

But the man didn't seem to believe her.

She sat down in a nearby chair and put her suitcase at her feet.

"A young girl getting on a train all by herself? Not to mention getting on a bus without anybody to help her, either."

Now that Madore mentioned it, Cassandra realized she hadn't hid the fact that she was a fairy very well.

"Fine. I'm an Air Fairy. If you don't mind, I'll be leaving now."

But as soon as she took a step away he grabbed her arm and shoved her into a nearby chair. "Okay, you probably have no idea who you're dealin' with here, dude. I could probably turn invisible and just walk away from you. Plus, you have absolutely no weapons on you, so I could kill you easily here with no witnesses. *Don't mess with me.*"

She growled, but as the last sentence came out the man pulled something from inside his cloak. It was a small, older piece of white wood. Thin, it gave the impression of being very delicate, but Cassandra knew it was harder than anything a human could make.

"You know as well as I do that this is a fairy wand, which finds its way, hopefully, to its chosen fairy. It is what every young fairy girl, like you, dreams of obtaining, though seldom do. I have the urge to give this to you, but you must promise in return that you will answer some of my questions."

"I swear on my honor as a fairy that I will answer Madore's questions. Now, please give me the wand so I can see if it's mine!" Cassandra eyed the wand hungrily.

More than once her father would have sat in his chair with Cassandra, who had been very little at the time, on his knee, telling her stories by firelight of great fairies with wands conquering all sorts of obstacles. It had been peaceful back when her father had been free; now all Cassandra wanted was to get him back.

"After you answer my questions. First of all, where are you going?"

"Earth Fairy Territory in Canada," Cassandra's eyes were still fixed onto the wand, but she pulled them away briefly to meet the man's eyes.

"Why?"

"My father was captured by the Dark Queen and friends of

his live up in Canada." Cassandra went on to explain who the Dark Fairy queen was, why she was evil, how those she ruled over lived in fear of her, and how she could track down anyone if they were outside long enough.

Finally, he nodded. "Okay, those are all my questions. So I guess this—" he handed over the wand—"is yours."

In Cassandra's hands the wand felt strangely warm, like there was a hidden power concealed in it. Lifting it high and steady, she pointed the foot-long piece of wood at a book and pulled with her mind to make it come to her. Indeed, the book slid out of the shelf and gently floated into Cassandra's outstretched hand.

"You're right; it is mine." Happiness flowed through Cassandra, from her head all the way down to her toes.

"Allow me to accompany you on your journey north," the man said.

"I don't sleep a lot; you may just hold me back."

He raised an eyebrow. "I'll sleep whenever I can get the chance, and you're a child journeying north by yourself. Just how odd do you think that would look to a normal person?"

"And you think it'll look better if I walk around with a strange man in a black cloak?"

"Don't get smart with me, kid!" The man roared the sentence with such ferocity that Cassandra jumped in surprise. "This may be a game to you, but to others it's a battle of life and death. I have to get out of here before a bunch of idiots find me and steal my soul, like they keep threatening to do, all because I found out about the secrets of YOUR KIND!" He said it as if it were a bad thing for fairies to even exist.

Cassandra was intrigued. She'd never heard of a creature that could steal souls. So how viable was Madore's story? Yet she was looking for a man being stalked by fairy hunters or other creatures of the dark. "Fine, but if you slow me down, it won't only be those strange people you'll have to deal with. I can kill you with a single blow, so don't even think about trying to hurt me."

When Madore's eyes flashed with fear for a second, Cassandra knew he had gotten the message.

They left the library and headed back to the train station, both staring straight forward, acting as normal as possible for a fairy and a man who knew mystical beings existed.

By now it was near midnight, and the train station only had one more train leaving for the north. But to their utmost relief, two tickets were still available.

Compared to the bus, the train looked brand new, though you could tell it had been running for a few years. Madore and Cassandra sat in a large, thirty-seat compartment, near the end of the train, far away from an elderly couple already seated so they wouldn't be overheard.

"We head north on this train till the sixth stop, then we should get out and try to find a subway that's still running."

It was a simple plan, but even the simplest of ideas had flaws. "What if the subway doesn't run this late at night?" she asked.

"Then we'll have to find some place to stay until it is running."

The lights inside the train flickered, as though all the light bulbs were about to go out at once. Then the lights went out permanently, and the train lurched forward to a shuddering stop. Cassandra, who hadn't been wearing a seatbelt, was thrown forward and hit her head on the seat in front of her before falling to the ground with a thud. Her suitcase lurched forward as well and hit her right shoulder, which immediately started to throb. Her glasses had fallen from her face, and she groped around on the ground for a few moments until she felt the cool, familiar metal of their frame. Dazed and confused, she sat there, trying to gather her thoughts.

When her head had cleared slightly, she stood and

concentrated her thoughts on her hand. The white light of an Air Fairy emitted from her fingertips, lighting the compartment. She nearly laughed with relief at what she saw: a little, light pink, fluffy, dog-like creature. It had at least the body, nose, and mouth of a normal dog, but instead of black pupils it had large silver ones. Seeing Cassandra, the strange thing hurtled over to her and jumped on her lap, content to start licking her face.

Luckily the old couple was sleeping. Madore simply stared.

As soon as the Mansuetus (for that was what the pink dog was called) saw Cassandra, the lights flickered on. After she laughed and pet the odd creature, the train slowly began to move forward once again.

"What is that?" said Madore, still staring at the little creature in shock.

"A Mansuetus can only be seen by those who believe in fairies. They feed off of energy, human and mechanical, until they find a fairy companion. That fairy companion alone knows the name to the Mansuetus," Cassandra said, reciting the definition from memory.

"Is fairy life always this complicated? I mean, you could probably search forever to find things like wands and Mansuetus, but few rarely find them."

"If you do find them, you were meant to have them. Besides, Mansuetus are not rare. They're common creatures that can be found all over the fairy world."

"So what's its name then?"

"Kiki and it's not an *it, she's* a girl." Cassandra said the Mansuetus' name as though she had known it all her life, when in fact she'd just learned it by looking into the little creature's eyes. When she said the little creature's name, she barked and licked Cassandra's face five times before turning in a circle and settling down on her lap.

"What does that wand of yours do anyway?"

"Basically what it did at the library—move objects." As she said it, Cassandra took the wand out of her suitcase, where she had been keeping it. The wand was quite magnificent for being only a half an inch thick, or at least that's how the wand looked to Cassandra. To Madore, a human, it looked like a plain little stick with white paint on it.

"I still don't see how you can find a dog but not a ride that will get us far north."

"You find me a holy place, and I'll get you a flying horse."

"A holy place?"

"Somewhere something religious has happened."

"Do I want to know why?"

"Unicorns flock to places like that, and I remember my dad showing me a poisonous bunch of berries they love that don't affect their hard stomachs."

"So the pointy-headed horses are real…well, I should have expected as much," said Madore, with an air of someone who could have a hot dog cart fly out of the sky and land on him and not be surprised.

"They're black horses during the day, that's why humans rarely ever see them, and those who do are believed to be mad."

"Well, I'm about to go mental if one more strange thing happens in my life."

"Then your sanity is not going to last long," Cassandra snipped.

For a while they lapsed in to silence. Madore shut his eyes, as if trying to get some sleep for the long journey ahead.

Cassandra, who had the window seat, stared out the window, trying to concentrate her magic so it would be there when she needed it.

All the things a fairy can do with their powers have never been counted. It depends on the type of fairy, seeing as their powers differ, like humans tend to have special talents, differing from arts to sports.

Cassandra's specialty was forcing things to become colder than they would naturally be. For her enemies, that meant if they tried gripping their weapon they'd probably never be able to use the hand the weapon had touched ever again.

Certain powers didn't come easily to Cassandra, which was normal for a fairy of her age and status. Flying while in human form was nearly impossible for her and controlling the wind usually ended up with disastrous results involving small hurricanes off the coast of South Carolina. In her fairy form, on the other hand, Cassandra could do all these things as easily as breathing.

Cassandra had fallen so deep into thought that she forgot how many stops had gone by. When the train's conductor announced their stop she jumped in surprise. After tapping Madore to wake him up, the two ran out the doors that had already started to close. This stop, unlike the last one, was crowded with people coming and going from jobs, which seemed odd, considering it was about three in the morning.

Some of the people, to her dismay, appeared to be illusions hiding a terrible creature. But she'd learned the hard way that these people were real.

As she looked off to the side, she ran straight into the man walking in front of her.

"Watch where you're going, kid," the large man with the long brown mustache and slight Southern drawl said. "You don't want to get in the way of people when they want out of a place."

"But why is everyone leaving?" Cassandra was surprised to hear herself asking the question of a complete stranger. Usually she would have simply nodded and kept walking.

The man looked her over, then evidently felt safe letting her in on the secret. "The police here don't believe what I'm about to tell ya, but the evidence was too overwhelming for the people here to ignore. People started disappearing: first the

Gregorys, then the McCarthy family. Others, too. About five families just upped and vanished without taking anything with them. Nobody even saw them leave on the train. The ticket salesman has no memory of selling them tickets, and their cars are all still at their houses. We haven't seen hair or hide of them for three months. Some families are afraid they've been eaten by a strange creature that growls loudly three times during the night all at specific times, and all the people can hear it. Everyone's terrified and not sure whom to trust, so they're leaving and not ever coming back. Me, too." With those words the man heaved two brown, battered suitcases and continued on his journey.

Turning to Madore, she said, "I'm going to assume it has something to do with my kind." But still she was puzzled as they walked out of the train station. Indeed, there was nothing she had ever heard of that could make sense of the creature apparently howling in the night. It could be a werewolf, she thought, but they were the kind of creatures who lived off small game they could find in the woods, not the sort of creature who would attack humans and drag them off to who knows where. Then there was the possibility that the two occurrences had nothing to do with one another, which seemed just as likely as the first solution. It didn't matter how much she looked and analyzed the situation, there was just not enough evidence to come up with a surefire answer.

"I say we forget the whole thing and keep heading north," Madore said.

Cassandra swiveled toward him in anger. "Fairy matters are dealt with by all fairies. You know, as well as I do, that it's our job to protect humans from magical harm. Besides, those weren't humans that were captured."

Her eyes looked solemnly at the ground as she chose her next words carefully. "The McCarthy family is a well-known family of vampires and the Gregorys, so I'm told, are elves."

Her glasses began to slip from her nose, and Cassandra pushed them up, knowing her world had just become a whole lot more complicated.

Four

This information put a whole new spin on the case in front of them. Now they could no longer ignore this odd tale, especially if innocent magic creatures were involved.

First, we better see just what's making this strange howling noise, thought Cassandra as she and Madore walked to a nearby gas station. She had to quicken her pace, though, because two of her steps equaled one of Madore's. Kiki bounced up and down in her arms, keeping perfect time with Cassandra's steps and every now and then snuggling up against her to get into a comfortable position.

The gas station seemed to be nearly deserted, except for the female cashier who was reading a magazine while talking to someone named "Jen" on her cell phone. Luckily she was so busy talking that she didn't seem to notice the strange teenager and cloaked man who walked in and hung around by the back of the store, trying to think of a plan.

"I say we listen to the howls during the night and try to find out where they're coming from." It wasn't the best plan Cassandra had ever thought up, but it was a plan nonetheless.

"Well, I was thinking we could ask around and see if anyone knows where the noise is coming from, because that'll cut our work in half."

When Cassandra agreed, they walked through town. Problem was, they couldn't find any people to ask. The stillness in the street was almost overpowering, for the only thing, you probably know, you can hear in a ghost town is your own beating heart. Cassandra's heartbeat was almost a steady hum, for fairy hearts are a lot stronger than human ones. But luckily for Cassandra, Air Fairies can't feel fear.

"Something is just not right," she said. "Like the fact that the clerk at the gas station is the only person here, and at her age she must live with her parents." As she spoke, Cassandra felt like she was stumbling headfirst into a huge clue that had been staring her right in the face. "So her parents must work somewhere, but the only people here are people who have inside jobs and don't have any kids running outside, unless they're all inside."

There were many creatures that could not have children. Most of them used magic to concentrate on a whole new being until it came to life, and when it did, it usually became as a teenager.

But then the ticket salesman at the train station had been an old, slightly wizened man....

Kiki shifted in her arms and Cassandra looked into the little silver eyes, feeling a stroke of inspiration coming on.

"You completely lost me, but you seem to think you're on to something, so I'll nod and act like I understand you." Madore did just that while Cassandra ran through every lesson she had ever learned, trying to find a creature that would fit the description laid out before them.

Nothing came to her, so they entered the grocery store. Black automatic doors slid back to reveal the same thing as the gas station—no people except for those that were working. A woman in her forties and two men that looked about ten years younger were sitting at their stations, each surrounded by merchandise. When they spotted Madore and Cassandra an odd look came into their eyes. They looked almost...hungry.

"Run!" Cassandra shouted to Madore. The usual fairy excitement rushed through her body as her adrenaline started to speed up.

Behind her a hideous scene began to unfold. The woman started growling, and the men quickly began to grow golden fur. A dark glow emitted from their bodies as the transformations began to take place. The shift from human to beast took no more than three seconds for each of them. When it was done, a cheetah and two large lions stood where there had once been humans.

The cheetah was gaining ground, slicing at the ground with her powerful legs....

☙❧

Madore, who was in pretty good shape for his age, began to fall behind Cassandra, breathing heavily. At the pace they were going, he wasn't going to make it. The cheetah was too fast, and he didn't have the same energy as a fairy did.

Human, fairy, and cheetah saw this and took action almost in the same instant. The slowest was Madore, who put on a burst of speed, like an athlete sprinting the last stretch before the finish line. Next came the cheetah, who also put on a burst of speed a lot faster than Madore's, so that now it almost looked like the large cat was simply flying through the air.

But Cassandra was the fastest by far. In the blink of an eye she was truly flying, up and away from the danger down below. Kiki and the suitcase were on her back, the little dog barking with excitement at the sudden rush of air, and Madore was hanging onto her arm, clinging hard so he wouldn't slip and fall.

When he saw what Cassandra had turned into, he nearly let go completely out of shock, and she had to reach down with her other arm to make sure he didn't fall to his death.

He had a right to be shocked. Anyone in their right mind would be shocked when seeing a fairy and their mark for the first time.

Every fairy, as I explained earlier, is almost the same, with their moon silver hair, eyes, and butterfly like wings. One thing I did not describe is what makes them different from each other. Their mark, which is usually some place like their arms, ankles, neck, and sometimes their faces, is like their fingerprint—no two are alike.

Cassandra's face was like a painted mask of blue and silver swirls, and in four places diamonds and sapphires were placed in perfect little circles. She would not have looked out of place at a Mardi Gras party.

The clothes she had been wearing had changed into Air Fairy robes, and her sneakers into the oddest pair of sandals, with knotted silver ribbons. Her rectangular glasses were missing. Wings emerged from two slits about a foot long in the back of her light blue robes and seemed to get smaller as they sloped downward and melted into the tough flesh of her back, which now had new muscles to accommodate the two pairs of large, silken wings. They beat with such efficient force they could keep both her and Madore up in the air with ease.

The town, the one they were now leaving, had been surrounded by a thick forest of trees. Now their tops resembled a small lake of green from their viewpoint a hundred or so feet above ground. About three miles away the trees began to shift as the ground below gradually changed from flat and smooth to mountainous. The first giant hill-like structure protruded from the land just a few miles away. It was smoother than the other mountains to the north and the green blanket of trees covered it in such a way that it looked like a giant green pimple on the smooth face of the land.

"Can we rest here?" asked Madore, as if desperate to get his feet back on the ground.

Cassandra laughed. She clearly was at ease in the sky. But she did as Madore had suggested and, holding on to his arms with both of hers, she dove downward. Cassandra whooped and hollered in joy, as Kiki hung onto her back. The suitcase was looped around her foot.

Madore yelped in surprise at the sharp dive and clung desperately onto his lifeline. In fact, he clung so hard that his fingernails dug into Cassandra's skin, breaking the soft flesh like butter so there were now ten small scars in semicircles on the girl's arms.

As both she and Madore dropped into a large oak near the very top of the mountain-hill, branches and leaves attacked their arms and legs, causing many scratches and bruises. Finally they both fell to the ground, Madore landing flat on his back while Cassandra, with the grace of an Air Fairy and Kiki and the suitcase now in her arms, landed perfectly on her feet.

When Madore looked up, he noticed something very odd about Cassandra. "Why don't you have any scratches?" He seemed to be covered with them, while the fairy's skin and wings weren't damaged at all.

"Watch." Cassandra drew in a breath of air, and silver sparkles began to emit themselves from her skin as she stored up energy. When she released the breath a shower of the sparkles landed on Madore, dissolving into his skin. As the sparkles dissolved, his skin began to heal itself. The process was over in the time it takes someone to blink, and when it was complete Madore's skin looked like it had never been scarred.

"Then how did you do that to yourself?"

"I blew upward, you idiot."

Madore feigned mock hurt at this, but stopped once he realized where they were.

It would be an understatement to say that the mountain-hill was a maze, because it was more like a labyrinth. Paths seemed to sprawl in every direction. If anyone tried to climb this puzzle of a mountain they would either get lost and starve to death or be forced to leave, unless, of course, they happened to have wings that could take them to the top.

"Something's not right," said Cassandra.

And he became aware of it, too. The mountain they were on seemed to pulse from an unknown source beneath their feet, like it was hollow and there was something underneath the surface. Kiki began to bark and growl with unease. The hair stood up on the back of Madore's neck. There were no animals on this mountain, not even the smallest cricket, and the silence was eerie.

"What should we do?" Cassandra began, then frowned. "Never mind, I know what *I'm* going to do. What *you* do is up to you."

"We're stuck with each other, so I think we should stay together."

Evidently it wasn't the answer Cassandra had been hoping for. "Great—just what I need, to get stuck with a man who knows about as much as a child would about magic."

They strode forward, Madore leading the way like he knew where he was going. They walked for about five minutes, their footsteps muffled by the surrounding silence. Strange marks adorned an oak to their left, a cedar to their right. All of this scared Madore and Kiki, who was now tucked snugly in her mistress's arms, but only intrigued Cassandra.

&

After they had walked awhile, another sight appeared in front of them as they moved through the maze towards it. The center of the maze hadn't been at top of the mountain, where Madore and Cassandra had just been; on the contrary, it seemed closer to the bottom of the western side.

Whatever it was sent out a force that pulled at Cassandra's soul, dragging her forcefully to it. Soon she could see plainly what it was: a giant hole. But this hole was unlike most holes in our world, for it seemed to plunge down forever into the blackness of space. Cassandra's fairy senses told her that the opening was the only entrance to hollow space inside the mountain. Her brain only had a few seconds to register this, though, because something else had happened that neither fairy nor human could have anticipated.

The clouds above the canopy had grown thick and dark, and rain began to pour downward, along with a small team of Dark Fairies. These fairies were even quieter than Cassandra and had the ability to blend into shadows as though they were invisible. Suddenly two sharp shoves sent both Madore and Cassandra, who was still holding Kiki and her suitcase, flying forward into the seemingly never-ending hole.

Cassandra's first impulse was to fly, as the rush of air hit at her body, but as she pulled her wings upward a ripple of pain shot through her tender wing muscles underneath her shoulder blades and she cried out. Staggering in the air, gliding downwards and not able to truly fly, she dove downwards toward the slight whistle of air that was Madore. She grabbed at where he supposedly was and caught hold of the hood of his cloak.

So with Kiki and her suitcase in one hand and Madore's hood, dragging her farther down the ever warming hole, in the other, it wasn't long before her arms began to feel numb from the strain of holding onto a fully grown man and a dog.

They glided like this for a few minutes, Cassandra sure that by now they were a bit of a ways below the Earth's surface. Finally they fell into a heap at the bottom of the hole.

"That was not the best landing I've ever seen," said Madore sarcastically, as he began to get up from the ground.

Both of them stopped when they saw what was looking at them—ten pairs of yellow and violet eyes. It was too dark in the hole to tell what the creatures were, but it was obvious they were the ones making the noises during the night.

Five

A pair of violet eyes, closer to the ground, meaning whoever they belonged to was young, was about to lunge forward. Cassandra could tell by his or her sudden movements.

"Don't, Caitlin," said one of the tall, yellow-eyed creatures, "they have an Air Fairy with them. I can tell from the smaller one's eyes. They're silver."

The purple-eyed Caitlin pulled back but still looked suspiciously at the two newcomers. To get a better view of the people in the hole, though Cassandra already had a suspicion as to whom they were, she concentrated all her thoughts and a slight soft white/silver glow emitted itself from her fingertips.

The cave was almost how Cassandra had been picturing it in her head, but with certain differences. It was round, approximately 50 meters in circumference, and the walls were fairly blackened moist earth with the occasional rock. On these walls were large scratches, where the inhabitants had probably gotten desperate, and larger rocks had been pulled from the walls to form makeshift chairs and tables. Obviously the occupants of the hole had a lot of time on their hands, because the rocks had been carved into chairs and tables by very small sharp claws.

The man who had told the young girl to stop looked at Cassandra and smiled. He was a fatherly gentleman, maybe in his early forties, and when he smiled at her it was with the reassurance a parent would show to their child. His hair was black with light gray streaks running through it, and he was almost on the sickly side of thin, though in the tunnel they seemed to have some sort of exercise program that the adults had enforced, because all of them were well muscled. Cassandra guessed that this was for if they ever had a chance to escape, which seemed highly unlikely, since the opening of the tunnel was so far away that it looked like a small star in a midnight black sky, and the walls weren't solid enough to climb.

The yellow eyes of the man in front of her immediately made Cassandra assume he was an elf. Indeed, when some of his hair swayed back, she could see the slight point to his ears that elves are very much known for. Humans wouldn't be able to notice if someone was an elf, not even if they looked very closely at their ears, because those who do not believe in magic cannot see it.

Next to him stood the young girl with violet eyes. Caitlin was tall, nearly as tall as Cassandra herself was, and her eyes, unnatural as they were, seemed gentle and almost sad. Dirty-blond hair fell about an inch past her shoulders in the front and in the back it was a few inches longer than that, and slightly curled at the tips. She had full cheeks, bright red lips, and her cheeks were lightly dusted with freckles.

When Cassandra turned her gaze towards Caitlin, the girl smiled, showing her teeth, which were gently glowing white, meaning she had had to straighten them with magic. Two fangs about an inch long sprang from her mouth when she realized Cassandra was looking at her. They overlapped her normal teeth and, unlike human beliefs, vampires could easily retract their fangs like a cat with its claws. The fangs were stored in the roof of the mouth until they were needed, and small muscles pulled back to release them and pull the small, dagger-like teeth back in.

Four other vampires stood in the crowd behind the two that were closest to Cassandra. By the way the mom and dad kept giving reassuring glances to the young twins of about six, whom they had stationed protectively behind them, you could tell they were a family. But they seemed to care nothing for Caitlin, who could have been in trouble if the strange people that just entered the tunnel hadn't been kind. Indeed it seemed the elf man, who took a defensive step toward her just in case, was more her family then those surrounding her.

The four other people in the crowd also had yellow eyes. One of them was obviously the mother and a son, of about sixteen, had put a reassuring arm around her and his little sister, who was about nine. Last was a man who wasn't standing, but sitting on one of the rock chairs and leaning on an old staff that was almost as decrepit as he was. He was like the older version of the elf man in front of them, his hair a white patch on his head while his skin was more wrinkled than flat.

Lack of sunlight had turned the elves' and vampires' skin white and they looked almost as haunted as ghosts, Cassandra was pretty sure that in five seconds they'd start moaning and saying they wanted to suck out her brain. When they saw the thin light Cassandra's magic made, they had to squint to get their eyes adjusted to it.

Their clothing made Cassandra want to cry. It was impossible to tell what color they were, or had been, seeing as there was dirt clinging to the cloth like it was magnetic. Mainly the men were wearing jeans and T-shirts, while the women, except for Caitlin, who was also wearing jeans like the men, wore almost floor-length skirts that were terribly ripped and short-sleeved blouses.

Kiki began barking at these strangers, and Cassandra stroked her gently to make her calm down.

"Please," said the man kindly, "come sit and tell us of news from the outside world."

He indicated one of five stone chairs stationed around a small stone table, which was nothing more than four large stones supporting a smooth, rounder stone. She took the indicated chair, which was to the left of the one the old man was sitting in. Madore sat on her right. The other two chairs were filled by the elf man and vampire, Caitlin. Others pulled chairs from the two other small tables and circled around, eager for any news. All eyes were on Cassandra, and she shifted in her seat uncomfortably.

"Not much has happened." Cassandra's voice shook a little as she spoke her next sentence. "People have been vanishing all over, but that's normal for the Dark Queen, and the town near here is overrun with cursed people."

At this the elf man cut in. "That we already knew of. The cat people took us from our homes to scare the townfolk away and to use the town as their own personal base, and from what you say it worked very well. But why did you end up here? From what you say I assume you used to live in the southern part of New York?"

Cassandra nodded, and the elf man continued. "That's very far from where we are now, as I'm sure you're aware of, and Earth Fairy Territory is to the north, which I'm also sure you're aware of. What's your story, young Air Fairy?"

At first Cassandra held her tongue and looked into the elf man's eyes, searching for some sign of a trap. Finding nothing, she took a deep breath and began her tale. She started from the time her father, Jacob Andrews, had vanished. When she said her father's name a flash of recognition passed over the elf man's face. But when she paused for him to speak he remained silent, and she felt it was possible she might have misread the expression, so she continued. She finished with Madore and herself falling down the tunnel. All the while Cassandra had been keeping the hole lit with light from her fingers. Finding this slightly annoying, Cassandra threw the light into the air, where it collected into a small ball hovering about ten feet off the ground.

"Dark Fairies pushed you down here," said the elf man, solemnly rubbing his eyes from exhaustion. Cassandra realized she had been talking quite a while and that the small light from the hole's opening was starting to fade. The two vampire twins, with their midnight black hair, sat on their parents' laps, sound asleep, and the young elf girl, who was sitting on her older brother's lap, was also off in dreamland. Kiki was also sleeping and, to Cassandra's embarrassment, slightly snoring. Caitlin looked like she was about to join those four, but she forced herself to stay awake.

"Why was I not able to fly?" The question had been nagging at the back of her mind ever since her awkward entrance into the tunnel.

"The air down here is filled with Dark Fairy magic, making it impossible for any of us to escape. Even if we climbed to the top of the hole, the magic would force us to fall back down again. We found that out the hard way," said the elf man, rubbing his back gently. Obviously he had tried to do just what he had described.

"I'm sorry to ask this, but who are you?" Cassandra looked around at the other people in the hole as she said this. She had a pretty good idea, but needed to ask all the same.

"We elves and Caitlin are part of the Gregory family."

Kiki suddenly switching positions in her arms wasn't what made Cassandra jump. The old man next to her had been silent up to this point, but now he spoke with a rough, almost British accent. "The vampires are from the McCarthy clan."

When Cassandra looked inquisitively at Caitlin, the old man gave a hoarse laugh that turned into a fit of coughs. After taking a few deep breaths, he was able to continue.

"My son adopted our dear Caitlin after his wife died, and my daughter—" he pointed to the young elf mother who sat next to her daughter and son and who looked nothing like the old man—"had Mary and Steven with a good-for-nothin' guitar player who ran off to be in a rock band."

A loud *whoosh* sounded throughout the hole, and Kiki

jumped in her arms. About eight loaves of bread and five tins of water came crashing down into the hole. One of them nearly hit Caitlin in the head, but it stopped abruptly in the air, along with everything else falling into the hole. The food began to glow silver and piled itself on the table in front of Cassandra. Caitlin muttered relieved thanks.

The old elf man began to chuckle. "Seems like it may be useful to have an Air Fairy around." Then, after getting that one sentence out, he began to cough again.

The elf man picked up the eight loaves and split them each in half. Everyone got a piece, and Cassandra took hers gratefully, not having eaten since the day before. She noticed that everyone ate slowly, trying to make every bite last as long as they could. Obviously they weren't fed often, and the water was even scarcer than the food. There seemed to be a routine of how things were done, because after the bread was eaten, the tin cans of water were opened. The vampires used their teeth like can openers, slicing the weak metal lid as though it was butter. The cans were passed around. When it was your turn, you were allowed one small sip. There were still four half loaves of bread left over, and these were again cut in half. Mr. Gregory, the elf man, handed out the pieces to everyone except himself, his sister, one of the vampire parents, and Madore, who had insisted that the elder gentleman should have it. After this they once again passed around the tins and took a sip, depleting their water supply. Kiki had to settle for licking tiny bits of water out of Cassandra's hand and eating some bread the fairy offered her.

As you've probably noticed, fairy folk can live with a lot less resources than normal humans. Cassandra hadn't slept for two days, and she was only just now beginning to feel tired.

"Having a fairy around also has some other advantages..." Cassandra grabbed her suitcase and reached down inside it. "Three apples!" she commanded, and three slightly bruised apples appeared in her hands. The Air Fairy handed the apples to the strong elf man, who split them all cleanly in two and passed the pieces around to the children. The kids laughed, even Caitlin, who acted more like an adult than a kid, and began munching on the apples as though they had never seen one before.

"I think we should all get some sleep before our nightly visitors arrive," said the old man, already half asleep himself.

At this, Cassandra let the light above them go out, plunging them all into darkness.

"Twelve blankets!" The wool blankets were in her hand before Cassandra had time to blink and she passed them to everyone in the room, who took them gratefully. One blanket was left over and Cassandra shrugged, sure she had just miscounted, and gave it to the two young vampire twins.

She curled up in a corner, Kiki sleeping down by her stomach to keep warm, five feet from the vampires and elves around her. At first she was too uncomfortable on the cold, hard ground to go to sleep, but soon exhaustion crept over her like a big, thick blanket. Her head was slightly spinning and sleeping on rock didn't help her looming headache.

☙❧

Cassandra was sure she'd only slept five seconds when someone roughly shook her arm. Kiki nearly barked in alarm, but Cassandra clamped a hand over the little dog's mouth.

Yellow eyes looked urgently into hers and she stood up silently. Cassandra and the person walked to the southeastern side of the hole, carefully trying to avoid stepping on sleeping elves and vampires. They sat at the table the vampire family had previously occupied.

Cassandra lit another light from her fingers, except this one was softer, so it didn't wake those sleeping not too far from the table. She wasn't surprised to find herself looking into the face of Mr. Gregory. Lack of sleep made the man before her look even older than he truly was, and his face was droopy, as though he was about to fall asleep at any second.

The young fairy jumped as someone moved swiftly from the shadows and sat down to her right. Caitlin had waited a few feet from the table, using her vampire ability of blending into the darkness, for Mr. Gregory to bring Cassandra over. The thirteen-year-old creature of the night no longer looked like she was going to pass out. On the contrary, she looked stronger then Cassandra had ever seen her. The night indeed magnified a vampire's powers.

"There's something I need to tell you both." Mr. Gregory's voice was just a hair above a whisper. "Cassandra—and yes, I know your name."

Cassandra was startled. Never once had she mentioned her name.

Mr. Gregory went on. "Cassandra and Caitlin, you two are very special, in a way your father and I hoped you'd never be. But a new situation has arisen, and I think it's time you learned why you are special."

Cassandra didn't dare interrupt, but a million questions had begun to pile up in her mind. She did her best to keep her mouth shut.

"Let me start from the beginning. There once was a man named Maxwell, who preferred the nickname *Maddy*, I might add. When he was young, Maddy fell in love with a young girl fairy named Kendra. He was the only thing that kept Kendra from going evil. Because, you see, the Dark King also felt Kendra was beautiful and decided to place a curse on the poor girl. Because Maddy had feelings for Kendra, he was able to stop the curse for a little while, but not long. When the Dark King saw this, he ordered Maddy to be killed. He escaped, but Kendra's mother wasn't so fortunate. Sadly, there was only one person Kendra could blame for this, and Maddy was on the run so couldn't defend himself.

"Thinking the two people she loved most in the world were gone, one being dead and the other she thought betrayed her, Kendra had no one left whom she felt cared about her. The horrible curse was able to take over her body completely. She married the Dark King and became the queen we know today."

Mr. Gregory stopped to take a breath after this, allowing one of Cassandra's questions to slip from her mouth.

"What happened to Maddy, and what do we have to do with this?" Cassandra had rushed through the sentence so fast that she was amazed Mr. Gregory had understood her.

"Patience, Cassandra," he said, smiling at the inquisitive fairy. "Maddy survived for a long time, and when your father," he looked pointedly at Cassandra, "and I met him, he had a crazy plan he was determined to put into action. Your father and I had been living next to each other at the time, and we learned magic together, so we were happy to help him.

"The young man had found out he could store the part of his soul that had fought against the dark curse surrounding Kendra. Then he could place that part of his soul within as many people as he wanted to. He decided to give it to your father, his girlfriend at the time, my girlfriend at the time, our best friend Josh, and myself. We now had the power to pass on the soul piece to whoever we wanted to. It seemed fitting, when we found out the Dark Queen was after us, and that she had found out through spies in the castle about the entire story, that we passed the power onto our children.

"Maddy disappeared after giving us the strong parts of his soul that held back a Dark Fairy curse, which had never been done before I might add. We assume he's either dead, imprisoned, or still on the run."

Mr. Gregory paused to let the information sink in and to see if they had any questions, and indeed they did have a few.

"So you put this dude's soul inside us?" Cassandra looked at Mr. Gregory as though he was completely out of his mind. When he nodded, Cassandra stared blankly at him. It took a few minutes for her brain to register the crazy tale that had just been told, but when she did she returned to questioning.

"You knew my father?" It wasn't the most important question in front of them, but Cassandra had to know.

"We were the best of friends, inseparable in our youth, but when we obtained our powers we could no longer stand to be near each other. For you see," he said solemnly, staring at the ground by his feet, "I got the odd part of the power. It kept shifting, and my moods would turn with it, to a point where sometimes even I couldn't control myself. Your father got the air part of the power, which was understandable, seeing as he was what he was. His girlfriend, who was not your mother," he added, seeing the question about to fall from Cassandra's lips, "was a girl named Tania who was a fierce Changeling; I'm assuming you both know what that is?"

Cassandra nodded in reply. That was elementary stuff for her, and she remembered her father teaching it to her as though it had happened just yesterday.

Changelings were odd creatures, with their ability to transform into any animal, human, or creature (like elves and fairies) by simply concentrating hard upon the wanted shape. It was impossible to tell if they were just in the shape they wanted to be in, or in their true form, the one they were born with.

"She was given the light piece of his soul and later married a human, for she wanted her child to know both of her parents, and marrying a human is the only exception for the rules regarding children only knowing one parental guardian," Mr. Gregory continued. "My old girlfriend Lea..." Once again he stopped, but this time he looked off into the distance, in some far off memory only he could see.

After a minute Cassandra cleared her throat, and he

snapped back to reality to finish his description.

"Well, she had the Earth part, an Earth Fairy if ever I've seen one, and Josh—" Mr. Gregory sighed heavily when he mentioned this name—"he thought he was a strong Light Fairy at the time, strong enough to take on the darkness of the last soul part, but even the strongest of men have fallen to the power of evil. Josh became hard and edgy. He loved to be around people, but only to find ways to manipulate them into doing his bidding. The good side of him began to put up a fight, and he didn't live to see his son, where the dark soul part now lives, grow up. Luckily for the child he grew up only knowing light and his mother helped make his soul strong from the moment he was born. He's probably had a much easier time holding the dark in than his father could ever have dreamed."

"Whoa, so hold on," Cassandra interrupted, "even if what you say is true, what do you expect us to do about it?"

"Find the other three children," Mr. Gregory said simply. "Bring the five pieces together and release the soul of Maddy on the Dark Queen to break her curse forever."

"But I thought you said Maddy's soul only held back the curse for a little while." At last Caitlin, who had been silent through the entire story, spoke.

Cassandra had assumed she had already known the story being told. But Caitlin seemed about as unaware as Cassandra was. Cassandra felt a stab of pity for the vampires. After all, what would it be like to have your own father tell a relative stranger a secret he'd been keeping from you your entire life?

But Caitlin didn't seem to mind at all, as though unexpected twists happened to her as frequently as they would in a fantasy novel.

"Come over here." Mr. Gregory stood and moved cautiously over to a spot big enough for the three of them, plus Kiki, to stand and for Cassandra to bring her light over without waking anyone. "Hold hands and stand as if you're a part of a

44

small circle meant for five."

They tried their best to do as he said and when they were finally in the correct position, they held their breath, unsure of what was going to happen next. Kiki had to sit on the ground at their feet and Cassandra was eager to pick her little friend back up again.

When Cassandra was almost sure nothing was going to occur, it happened. Light began to surround the two girls and grew in intensity until it was so bright they were forced to shut their eyes. Those who were sleeping woke with a start and were also forced to snap their eyes to shield them from the blinding light. Kiki started barking and ran to one of the vampire twins, who shielded her in his arms. A crack like that of a whip shook the tunnel with such force that the elf mother screamed in terror, afraid rock would fall down and suffocate them all. But the crack went as quickly as it had come, leaving everyone with a horrible headache. Slight humming could be heard as the light from Cassandra and Caitlin began to die down.

But it wasn't over yet. Part of a dark ring, like there was a hoola hoop overhead and this was its shadow, filled the space where three other people should have been standing. Something began to take shape in the middle of the circle, a strange mass that couldn't be distinguished as anything, and as seconds passed it began to take on its true form. The thing was a star; three of its points were still dark shadow while the other two were made of only white light. Cassandra assumed the middle and the three dark parts would only light up when all five pieces of the soul were brought together.

When Caitlin and Cassandra finally broke from the circle, the star and the semidark ring vanished.

"Any more questions?" asked Mr. Gregory, as though nothing had just happened.

"Yeah, one," said Cassandra sarcastically. "Why did you wait until we were trapped inside a hole to tell us this?"

The elf man did not reply but instead looked down at his sneakers, which were battered beyond repair. He took a deep breath and reluctantly met Cassandra's strong, sturdy gaze. "We didn't think it was time until it was too late."

Cassandra interrupted. "I'm assuming you mean that my dad didn't tell me before he got captured and you weren't planning on getting trapped in a hole before you had time to tell your daughter about her gift."

Mr. Gregory nodded sadly. "Well, now that everybody's awake, I think we should all go back to sleep."

Cassandra didn't see much sense in this sentence, but the old man smiled like he had just said the answer to one of life's largest mysteries.

Indeed Cassandra would like to have fallen asleep right then and there, but forced herself to remain awake, if just for a few minutes longer. Something someone had said was beginning to stir in her mind and for the longest time, no matter how hard she concentrated, she couldn't figure out what it was. Finally it came to her in the sudden flash a fairy always has when they remember something a human would normally forget.

"Mr. Gregory," Cassandra asked, "what did your father mean when he said 'our nightly visitors'?"

"You'll see soon enough." The reply was dark, as though Mr. Gregory was going through a violent mood swing. Cassandra realized this is what he meant when he said he had gotten the odd part of the soul. It must be even harder for Caitlin, she realized, because the girl now had that part of the soul. Even though it had had a lasting effect on Mr. Gregory, having the soul must feel a lot worse.

Cassandra had never felt her gift, which is probably why she never knew it was there.

What happened in front of them made Cassandra feel the man in front of her was not crazy—quite the opposite, though he may be a little mad after having the odd piece of the soul.

As she looked around at the sleeping elves and vampires, another question tingled on her lips. "Where's Madore?" She hadn't seen him in quite some time.

The silver light above them couldn't stop the shivers that began to run up everyone's spine as someone entered the hole.

"Why, I'm right here." The voice wasn't Madore's, for it was cruel and merciless, as though the person could watch someone kill themselves and not bat an eyelash. Cassandra spun around, her gentle fairy feet hardly making a noise on the rocky ground.

The sight was a horrible one to behold, and Cassandra had to hold back a gag. Kiki, who had jumped back into her mistress's arms, was too scared to even bark. The little dog began to shiver uncontrollably.

Dark Fairies are despicable, that much I have made clear, and they are quite gross. Air Fairies take pride in being clean, but Dark Fairies would much rather be dirty.

Dirt encrusted their midnight-colored clothing, which consisted of a pair of jeans, a tunic (which clashed horribly with the jeans), black penny loafers, and cloaks fastened by black jade broaches. Their wings hardly needed to be attached to their bodies. They were hardly wings at all—more like shadows that were able to manipulate the wind around them. The only reason you could tell the wings were there at all was because they were darker than the shadows around them. Their marks had no jewels and glitter like the marks Air Fairies were known for but were basically black paint. Six pairs of cold, black eyes stared into Cassandra's silver ones.

The nearest one was rat-faced and familiar, but now he looked about the age as Cassandra. At Cassandra's surprised expression he laughed, took a bottle of blood-colored liquid from the inside of his cloak, and sipped it. There was a noise, like someone slamming on the brakes of a car to come to a sudden stop, as his body lurched forward. In the second he had before landing, his form changed into the familiar shape of Madore.

Now Cassandra realized why her old companion had always worn a black cloak.

"Four words, little Air Fairy." The cold voice, which sent a chill up Cassandra's spine, hissed, "Never…talk…to…strangers…"

Madore laughed as he stepped back into his own shape.

Six

The Dark Fairy assistant, Corner, was done playing games with the pathetic creatures in front of him. It was time for business, and they knew it as well as he did. Without his queen striking fear down to his very core, even though fairies can't fear for themselves, the Dark Queen was able to strike down her subjects with threats about relieving them of their positions. So Madore—who was really Corner—stood tall and held himself with the slight air that said he was better than everyone else.

"Which of you has the soul?" A sneer spread across his lips when he didn't get a reply. The fairies behind him looked like zombies, there eyes gazing forward, seeing but not really taking anything in.

He did on the other hand hear the comment Cassandra directed at Mr. Gregory.

"So you aren't crazy!" She said it with as much sarcasm as she could and now she was going to pay the price, as she noticed the look Corner was giving her. His brows creased and one side of his lip began to twitch with utter hatred. He smelled the strong magic, which every creature except humans gave off, surrounding her....

⊱⊰

Madore, or whoever he was now, reached out so quickly that Cassandra didn't have time to think of a spell to counter the attack. All of a sudden an invisible giant wrapped itself around her body, crushing her beneath its mighty force. Madore lifted the invisible thing in his hand, and Cassandra shot upwards so fast, she gasped as the air was knocked from her body. The sneer was still on his face as he tossed the Air Fairy around with dark magic.

This must be what it's like to be a baseball. The young fairy wanted to scream. Her head felt it was about to explode as her neck was whipped around in very uncomfortable ways and she didn't have enough air in her lungs.

Finally the Dark Fairy got bored and tossed Cassandra aside, where she was able to adjust her wings to catch most of her weight before landing roughly on her feet.

Cassandra had landed right next to Caitlin. The young vampiress grabbed Cassandra's hand as she began to involuntarily sway from the harsh landing. Still in shock from the rough handling she'd been forced to endure, Cassandra wasn't able to think straight...or to give Madore a taste of his own medicine. The people around Cassandra wanted to help...but they couldn't.

"If none of you talk, that's fine by me," Madore said.

Another chill ran up Cassandra's spine at these words.

"Just remember, you hand over the person with that stupid man's soul, and the rest of you get to go free." A high, merciless laugh filled the hole as the Dark Fairies vanished into the shadows.

"That wasn't nearly as bad as it usually is!" the crazy old man said cheerfully. Through the entire show he had sat silently in his chair, not moving for fear of the Dark Fairies spotting him as the only one sitting and deciding to punish him for it.

Cassandra's legs begged to differ as they groaned in protest, forcing her down to her knees. She was too tired to ask the questions that had bubbled up to her lips. Before she had time to think about what she was doing, she fell into a deep sleep....

50

The night passed in a fit of terrifying dreams for the young fairy. The Dark Fairy's face kept appearing, changing into Madore's and back again. Then her father would appear, smiling happily at her, unaware that the Dark Fairy was right behind him. The Dark Fairy behind her dad grinned wickedly, and Cassandra knew she had to warn him before something horrible happened. But it was if she were frozen, glued into place by some invisible power. She feared being forced to watch her father's death. Luckily, before anything else could happen in the dream, she would wake up in a sweat, with her robes and silver hair clinging to her body, screaming.

❧❦

By far, Cassandra's screams from her nightmares were the most terrifying noise the people in the hole had ever heard. The elves and fairies woke every time the disturbing noise arose in the air. After the sixth time the old, Elvin man walked over to Cassandra and hit her precisely in the back of the head with the larger part of his staff. When she fell asleep this time, she didn't dream and didn't wake up until very late in the day, making Caitlin fear that her grandfather had hit her too hard.

Caitlin wasn't surprised that Cassandra's first encounter with the Dark Fairy, the Dark Queen's assistant, Corner, had been so troubling.

Finally around one o'clock Cassandra's eyelids fluttered open, reminding Caitlin vaguely of Sleeping Beauty, and the fairy groaned at the pain throbbing in her back temple. When she learned what had happened from Caitlin, she glared at the old elf man so hard a normal human would have cowered in fear. But the old elf just smiled and rocked back and forth on his chair.

Later on, when the pain had subsided from her head, Cassandra apologized and thanked him. When he told her it was no trouble and that he'd gladly hit her again tonight, Cassandra scowled and walked away.

~·~

There wasn't much going on that day, and the cramped space made life nearly unbearable. Cassandra's magic was going berserk and when the morning meal came raining down upon their heads, she was just able to get it to the table, but accidentally hit Caitlin upside the head with a loaf of bread. The vampiress didn't seem to mind, but five seconds later she had a mood swing and hit Cassandra on the arm as payback. Ten seconds later she apologized and told her it was the odd part of the soul working its magic again. When she heard the word *magic* Cassandra realized what she had wanted to ask the day before.

"Why did that Dark Fairy—" Cassandra did not yet know Corner's name—"give me a wand if he wanted to trap me in this...awful place?"

"Wand? Let me see your wand!" Mr. Gregory turned in half lap (they had been running laps to keep in shape) and stopped so abruptly that Cassandra ran into him.

The Air Fairy walked over to her suitcase, which had been lying in a corner where she slept and served as her pillow during the night.

The thin, white stick looked plain as ever. Mr. Gregory relaxed after he had whispered some strange words, which Cassandra took to be an elf spell.

"The Dark Fairy is Corner, the Dark Queen's assistant. The wand probably masked his fairy magic. If you were to have looked him over to see if he was a fairy, you would have assumed any magic he had was because he had the wand for a short while. Plus it was a great way to make you trust him."

Cassandra nodded and finished her last lap.

That night the old man did not fulfill his promise to knock out Cassandra. Their horrible visitors didn't come, which was odd, Mr. Gregory voiced aloud, because they usually came every night.

So Cassandra slept, but not nearly as peacefully as she would have liked. Dreams still plagued her sleep, and there was no cure for it, except to wait it out.

"They used to take one of us out of the hole completely and try to torture or persuade the information out of us." Mr. Gregory shuddered at the thought.

"One of the townsfolk said they heard noises at certain times during the night!" Cassandra said, remembering the words of the man at the train station.

"That would be the Stevens," replied Mr. Gregory.

Cassandra nodded in recognition of the werewolf name.

"They're trapped in a hole somewhere," Mr. Gregory continued, "though we can't tell exactly which one."

"The Dark Fairies know someone in this area has the soul, but they're not sure who." Caitlin had heard Mr. Gregory and Cassandra talking and decided to join in on the conversation. "Not that it matters, seeing as they've trapped everyone possibly holding onto it."

Cassandra felt like she was a train who had just run straight into a brick walls. There were no clues now to follow…and no way to get out of the prison she'd been stupid enough to fall into. But there had to be a way…

☙❧

Their chance to escape came that night.

Cassandra was curled up with Kiki, once again where they normally slept. She had been struggling through another nightmare, her body shaking from the stress of it all and her hair once again glued to her face by sweat. Lately it had been unbearable to sleep and the longer she prolonged falling into the fit of overwhelming screams and terror, the harder the dreams were.

This night Kiki had been trying to comfort her mistress, licking her face and curling up in her arms....

〜•〜

The little dog barked as the familiar face of Corner leaped out of the shadows. Caitlin heard it before anyone else and crept silently into the darkness next to where Cassandra was sleeping. Corner was tying her arms down with magic.

Cassandra awoke with a start.

"We're gonna see if our new little fairy friend will let us in on a little secret," mocked Corner as he began to lift Cassandra, and Kiki to her dismay, once again in the air.

Little did he know a young vampiress, in her invisible state, had wrapped her arms around Cassandra's waist, so when Corner pulled them upward, Caitlin went with them.

There was a *swish* as an Air Fairy, vampiress, mansuetus, and Corner flew upward through the air. Caitlin felt she was going to be sick, as the rush of air hit her stomach hard and her body began to whip around uncomfortably. The creature of the night had to bite down on her lip to stop herself from crying out and giving away her position as her hands began to slip from Cassandra's waist. But she held on, like a drowner clings on to anything buoyant. Another problem was Cassandra's wings, the bottom pair about an inch from her head, which kept whacking her hard in the face and threatened to force her to lose her grip.

Cassandra seemed to be frozen stiff, unable to respond except to stare into the cold, dead eyes of Corner.

Last but not least was Kiki, who clung onto Cassandra's robes with her claws. The little puppy had her head down, fighting against the air rushing around her, not having enough strength to bark.

They reached the opening of the hole just as Caitlin and Kiki were nearing the end of their strength.

Even under the familiar canopy of trees the night sky above them was one of the most relieving sights the three of them, especially Caitlin, who hadn't seen it in a while, had ever seen. The stars ahead were just tiny beams of light in endless darkness.

"It looks nice, doesn't it?" mocked Corner as he released Cassandra from the magic of holding her up, causing her to fall down upon Caitlin, who once again had to bite her lip so she didn't cry out in pain. "You can go if you want to. But we'd both know what you'd be leaving behind. You'd go free, but all hope of saving your father would be gone."

☙❧

Cassandra was careful not to step on the already hurt Caitlin (for she had sensed her friend was there).

"Yes I know about your father," Corner said, as if enjoying hurting her. "He's an honored guest at the dark queen's castle." When a cruel smile played across Corner's mouth, Cassandra knew her dad wasn't being treated well. "Your father didn't have the soul piece, so we made an assumption that you had it. From that look in your eyes…"

Cassandra hadn't sensed her eyes had changed from the hard, poker-player-like expression she'd adopted, but she let Corner continue all the same.

"…I can tell we were correct. But, you see—" the Dark Fairy gestured down towards the hole—"we don't know who has the soul down there. However, if you go it doesn't matter, because you alone can't complete the spell, so you're no threat to us. So what's it going to be? Leave this place and your hopes behind? Or stay and be trapped in this hole forever?"

Now Cassandra saw what Corner was doing. If she hadn't landed on top of an invisible person, she'd probably feel terribly hurt and confused by these words. That was what he wanted—to torture her not only on the outside, but also on the inside.

Cassandra knew her choice was clear.

Corner continued to eye her suspiciously. Then, sensing somehow that she wasn't alone, the Dark Fairy lashed out.

Cassandra dodged out of the way of the oncoming shadows invoked by Corner, which hurled themselves as hard as they could toward their victims and shrieked with the voices of Dark Fairies long deceased.

Caitlin screamed and became visible as she clung hard to the flying Air Fairy. Kiki was too scared to do anything, so she buried her head in Cassandra's robes.

Suddenly the wind around them intensified and hit Corner so hard that it knocked the air from his body and flung him backwards into a tree. He retaliated by trying the levitation spell once again on Cassandra but missed continuously as the swift Air Fairy began a weaving pattern around a clump of trees. After a few dodges, Cassandra jumped out and hit Corner on the back of the head. He crumpled to the ground, knocked out cold.

Caitlin found her voice. "What are you going to do? It's not like we can just leave him here and let him get Dark Fairy reinforcements."

Cassandra thought that over as Caitlin stared at her, waiting for an answer. "Don't tell anyone I did this. It's against fairy code to attack a sleeping victim."

"But that's what he did to you!" Caitlin exclaimed.

"Well, he's not a very good fairy, now is he?" replied Cassandra in an unmistakably sarcastic tone.

She touched the unconscious fairy in the back of the head, trying not to retch as she felt his greasy hair, and forced herself to calm her mind to make it easier to slip into her magic, even though she was on the verge of vomiting from his overwhelming stench. A light, silver as usual, appeared at her fingertips. It glowed there, under her skin, for a fraction of a second before dissolving underneath Corner's skull and into his brain, where it could no longer be seen. Five seconds later the light returned to the Dark Fairy's skull and dissolved back into Cassandra's fingertips, before vanishing completely.

Cassandra's brows furrowed in concentration, and tiny beads of sweat formed on her forehead as she held on to her magic. "Go invisible and hold on to me!" Cassandra hissed to Caitlin.

A grim smile played upon Corner's lips as he began to rise. "Go on, then, do what you please."

Cassandra flew upwards, clutching Kiki to her chest. She hoped desperately that Caitlin could hold on for a little while longer since, at this point, her strength had to be fading.

Cold, cruel laughter filled the night air as Corner watched them leave. *The last hope for the creatures of light is gone*, a voice inside Corner's head whispered to him, *and now nothing can stand in our way.*

Seven

"What just happened?" said Caitlin, as they landed in a nearby town (not the one that was cursed, because that would be stupid on their part) twenty minutes later. She felt like she was on the verge of throwing up, so she tried to take as many deep breaths as possible to calm the swell rushing up into her throat. Flying wasn't something she wanted to do again for a while.

"I should be asking you the same thing," Cassandra said as she nearly tripped getting onto the curb of the road. She grinned at Caitlin.

"I turned invisible when I heard the guy come in," Caitlin said modestly, having seen Cassandra's grin and knowing that they wouldn't have been able to pull this off if it wasn't for her own quick thinking. "It wasn't much, and I wasn't thinking…"

"Sometimes being impulsive can be a good thing," said Cassandra, gesturing around them. "It freed us, didn't it?"

"But what happened when you worked your magic on that Dark Fairy? I know fairies can't steal memories or alter them at all, so then what did you do?"

"It's my favorite spell in the world," Cassandra explained, "called 'Air Fairy Dreams.' When he was knocked out, I was able to take on a form familiar to him. I assumed he was a loyal servant to his queen, so I took on her form. I told him the person hanging on to me was a Dark Fairy, and when I was farther away and thought I was safe, that person would kill me. You should have seen him." She laughed. "He nearly fainted with fear when he saw the Dark Queen showed up all of a sudden!"

But Caitlin didn't laugh. Something else was on her mind. "Corner feared for his life?" It was something unheard of for a fairy, even for one as despicable as Corner.

At those words Cassandra's brows furrowed. Uncertainty filled her eyes. Finally she shook her head, like a dog trying to rid its ears of water. "It's impossible, unless—" a knowing look dawned on her face—"he was acting, like when he was Madore."

Both Air Fairy and vampiress turned around, to see shadows appearing above the mountain they had just left. They screeched with an unearthly pitch, sending shivers up their preys' spines, and began to dive forward, along with their Dark Fairy masters. The chase was on, and both girls turned on the spot and sprinted forward on the sidewalk. But few things on the ground can match the speed of flight, and their pursuers were flying.

Little did Cassandra realize, as she pushed herself forward as hard as she could, that she too could have flown. Her silver wings were clamped together, making it easier to run forward, and if another Air Fairy had been around, Cassandra would surely have been punished for not using them to get away.

No one was on the sidewalk. All of the townspeople must have been safely at home sleeping. Stone made unpleasant crunching noises as their feet struck the ground hard, sending shock waves up the girls' legs. Cassandra's chest was heaving up and down by this time. Caitlin was no better off as she clutched KiKi to her chest.

"We've got...to get to...an enclosed building," said Cassandra, her breath coming in short, painful gasps.

Seeing the fear in the Air Fairy's eyes, Caitlin wondered, at first, if Cassandra feared for her own life. Then the realization hit her. *It's me she's fearing for.* Touched that an Air Fairy would care about a vampiress, Caitlin put on a burst of speed to catch up to her new friend.

It was an unfortunate time to be looking for a building to enter, since the shops in the town were all closed at this time of night, but the Dark Fairies weren't that far behind. The young vampiress wanted to cry out in pain, as her legs, thighs, ankles, and feet burned with such intensity that a human would have passed out if forced through what Caitlin was now experiencing. Terror kept her going, and it was terror that was probably saving her life.

Sadly, even though she was a tough creature of the night, it was all too much for the vampiress, as her legs gave a loud moan. When she tried to put her foot down again, she slipped and was forced to reach forward with the other leg. This time both legs didn't support her weight, and she tumbled to the ground, unconscious....

ॐ

"NO!" Cassandra screamed, as her friend was swarmed by dark, merciless shadows. She turned, the wind around her becoming stronger as she blasted wildly, shots of air flying as hard as cannonballs toward the oncoming swarm of darkness. But shadows aren't solids, and the air passed harmlessly through their darkness and hit buildings behind them, with enough force to break some of the bricks and wood into small piles of rubble. The families inside were obviously too deep in their sleep to notice, and Cassandra envied them as her enemies once again began to advance.

Pain tore through her body like a knife through a thick slab of butter. She knew she was on the verge of passing out, but that, if she did so, her fate was sealed, so she struggled to stay awake against the horrible burning sensation filling her body. She stumbled forward in a desperate attempt to reach her unconscious friend, but fell, knocking the wind out of her chest as she hit the stone. She didn't have the energy to get back up.

Kiki was no better off, as the small pink dog whimpered in pain while falling to the ground, which probably would have killed a normal dog. Cassandra could barely feel the dog licking her face, but it kept her awake for the half a second she desperately needed.

That's when Cassandra saw Caitlin's hand, about a yard from her own burning fingers. It was the only part of her friend she could see, the rest being covered in Dark Fairy shadows as they tried desperately to kill, slowly but surely, both their victims. Cassandra had an impulsive thought, as she saw the hand just lying there, and decided to see if an impulsive action would save them once again.

Cassandra pushed her hand, her arm muscles receiving a horrible shot of agonizing pain that threatened to knock her into the black abyss of unconsciousness, toward the pale hand of the vampiress covered in shadows. When she was close enough, and the blackness of sleep was almost unbearable to look at and not fall into, Cassandra let her hand drop towards her friend's as the darkness finally consumed her.

⌘

The white light of Maddy's soul began to glow around both the unconscious victims, and the shadows screamed in horror as their tasty prey now had the sole thing they feared—light—surrounding them. Caitlin heard these screams of terror just when Cassandra's hand began to slip away from hers. Instinctively she grabbed Cassandra's palm.

Just over the horizon another light was coming—this one intense enough to shine upon half the world.

The Dark Fairies didn't think twice as they commanded their shadows to fly west of them, away from the brilliance of the sun. Caitlin gave a relieved sigh as she watched them go.

Then, still tired from the harsh run, she pulled her hand from Cassandra's and fell back to sleep.

This probably wasn't the smartest thing to do, since now the two girls were at the mercy of whoever decided to go down the little sidewalk they were on. Luckily the only person up early in the little town on that day was the paper boy. He was riding his bike on the street, not paying attention to anything but where he usually threw the newspaper.

It's an odd thing, indeed, when you are awakened from twenty minutes of sleep by a flying newspaper. In fact, I'm pretty sure it has only happened on accidental occasions, unless your sole purpose in life is to be hit upside the head with newspapers in odd places.

The paper boy stared at the two girls with the look of someone who had just been hit over the head with a baseball bat, then peddled onward as the fairy and vampiress behind him pulled themselves up into standing positions.

Caitlin and Cassandra's shoulders sagged as the stress of last night pressed down upon them. At first their thoughts were so fuzzy that all they could do was lean on one another and try to remain standing. Then they realized they somehow needed to get inside, just in case their enemies decided they wanted to come back. This was difficult, seeing as they were in a small cul-de-sac full of houses and would probably not find a hotel for some distance. It was also impossible for them to get a taxi in a suburban area, since neither of them had a phone. And a long walk was out of the question, since they were so weary.

But if the residents stepped out of their houses to find two strange girls on the sidewalk and their houses damaged, they'd obviously become suspicious.

The young fairy, feeling another slight boil arise in her blood at the mere thought of a chase, pulled Caitlin away from the cul-de-sac with renewed strength. But that energy began to fade as they found their way onto a main road leading toward a bunch of oddball shops that included everything from a place to buy masks to a place to eat French fries. Many times the pair stumbled and had to lean on each other for strength.

If it was night time, Cassandra thought, realizing they could have done this last night if she had been thinking, they could have flown. After all, Caitlin, being in her invisible state that she could only accomplish in darkness had made it to a hotel in no time. But now here they were—powerless, weak, and hungry. All they could do was keep going, even though it hurt, and even though Cassaandra wanted so desperately to fall back into the soft, comforting blackness of sleep. One step...two...a stumble...another step. The work felt monotonous as their legs burned with the effort of keeping up their body weight.

Finally Cassandra fell to her knees, surprisingly enough, seeing as she, being a fairy, should have been the stronger of the two. Her glittery eyelids, which were also part of her fairy mark and were covered in permanent blue and silver paint, were beginning to close...until Caitlin roughly shook her awake.

There wasn't much of a place to rest. Only a back alley (which wasn't even an option), a furniture store with a young couple shopping for sofas, a nearly deserted café except for a worn-out waitress, and a barber shop with four guys warming up their voices to sing all day. Caitlin dragged Cassandra towards the door of the furniture store, and they sank down next to the windows, against the cool, hard brick.

Ten minutes later, after they had both taken quick naps, the girls moved on, their legs feeling like spaghetti as they took one step after another.

"A bus stop!" Cassandra cried in delight as she saw the familiar bench and sign. They sat down, wondering if their legs could even move when the bus came. Then a thought hit Cassandra. "We don't have any money," she said in despair.

She looked around desperately for her suitcase, knowing it

was hopeless because she had left it back in the hole.

Caitlin groaned and held her head. "Why didn't those fairies finish us off?"

Cassandra pondered this thought for a long time, then finally said, "They can't come out during daytime, and they might want us to suffer a long journey searching everywhere for three people they've most likely captured!" The full weight of the situation now rested on her stomach. "This is not only a chance to rescue my father; it's a chance to help a lot of fairies who are being tortured. But the Queen's has to have made some plan to stop us; it can't be so easy. Can it?"

Caitlin shook her head.

Then, exhausted, they both dozed off as they waited for the bus.

☙❧

When the bus came, Cassandra and Caitlin got on, only not in the usual way, because the girls sat on the rear bumper. An old lady in a passing car saw them and almost veered off the road in amazement. Cassandra and Caitlin laughed at her stunned expression, then nearly fell off the bumper and underneath the wheels of the car behind the bus.

They got off when they saw a huge sign reading *Hotel*. Not that they could get a room, seeing as they were broke.

Cassandra hoped that once they were inside the hotel she'd think of something, but it was Caitlin who came up with the brilliant plan.

It was a nice building, with a plush carpet and high domed ceiling. The only person working was a small, gray-haired woman working at one of three computers, obviously meant for people to check in.

"Do you believe in vampires?"

Cassandra couldn't believe Caitlin had just walked up to

the old lady at the check-in counter and asked that. Cassandra trailed behind her friend, hoping there were no fairy hunters around.

"Sure, hon."

Caitlin had laid the cute, innocent act on so thickly that the old lady, who reminded her slightly of the elf grandfather she had left behind in the hole of a prison she had escaped, must have thought she was just a cute, innocent street girl, who must have had a hard life, seeing the state of her and her clothing. But Caitlin hated being called "hon," even by a wrinkled old lady.

All of a sudden Caitlin's smile turned into a broad, toothy grin, which grew as her two fangs began to slide into position. The lady didn't even have time to scream before she fainted in fright. Both Air Fairy and vampiress felt bad, but all thoughts of pity vanished at the thought of two soft beds to sleep in.

Now it was Cassandra's turn to make a plan, as she touched the old lady's head, which was a good deal less greasier than Corner's. A familiar light sank into the woman's head and then came back. Not too long after the old lady began to stir, her eyes fluttered open.

"Well then," she said breathlessly, obviously astonished at what had just happened, "I'll get you girls a room for a week with two beds. Breakfast is served here at nine every morning." She pointed toward a hall leading off to the right that opened into a room with metal chairs and tables covered in white cloth.

The lady hit a few keys on the computer in front of her, then pulled two room cards from underneath her desk. "Is there anything else I can do for you?" she asked pleasantly, as though nothing strange had just happened.

"Yes, ma'am," said Cassandra, just as kindly, "what time is it?"

"Why it's eight o'clock, dear," the woman replied, smiling.

Cassandra took the two room cards and walked down the

hall, past the breakfast room, then found an elevator. Since entering the hotel both vampiress and fairy had forgotten the pain of extreme exhaustion. Now, as they entered the elevator, which was empty this early in the morning, their adventures in the night caught up to them and they slumped onto the elevator's red carpet without a second thought.

The annoying ding that announced their stop came too soon in their opinions. But Cassandra forced herself up and half dragged, half helped Caitlin to her feet. Their room card was for number 436, and the hall they stepped out into started with room 390. So, once again leaning on each other for support, the girls began to trudge unwillingly towards their room. When they finally got there, they were on the verge of collapsing. It took Cassandra three tries, as her arm refused to do what her brain told it, to slide the card through the door lock the right way. But on the fourth try it finally gave a satisfying *click!*

Cassandra pushed the door forward, nearly falling flat on her face in the process, into a nicely furnished room. The two beds looked so warm and inviting. There was also a desk, two large windows that took up one side of the room and were covered in vanilla-colored blinds, a bathroom that led off from the main room through a small door, an oak chair, and a matching table.

"What did you do to that lady at the front counter?" Caitlin asked.

"I gave her a dream in which she fainted and we yelled for help and then she woke up and felt fine. You didn't have fangs, so it was like nothing happened and she just hallucinated that you were a vampire. Then we paid for our rooms and that was the end of the dream. It was quite funny, actually."

"There's something we've go to do tomorrow..." Caitlin's voice began to fade as she fell onto the bed and almost immediately into a deep slumber.

"We've got to find the Changeling." Cassandra forgot why

she said this as she placed Kiki on her bed, but she knew it was important. By the time her body landed on the bed, she was already asleep.

Eight

Caitlin woke up first, shivering. She'd slept in a cold air-conditioned room all midmorning and a good deal into the afternoon without bothering to put on a comforter, unlike Cassandra, who was still sleeping soundly under a thick blanket on the bed next to Caitlin's. Visions of that night reminded Caitlin where she was and why she was there.

Grumble.

Her stomach moaned from lack of food, but Caitlin took no notice, having lived in a hole for a month with nearly nothing to eat, so minor stomach pains weren't a problem for her. Cassandra shifted in her sleep, pulling Kiki, who had slept next to her master's head, close to her and reminding Caitlin vaguely of a little girl sleeping with her doll.

Caitlin leaned back against the headboard, forgetting her hunger pains and willing herself to go back into the gentle stillness of sleep.

Grumble.

Caitlin had cried the first time she had felt the strong hunger pains in the first week of living in the hole. Her elf father had tried desperately to comfort her as the pains gnawed at her insides, almost forcing her to throw up the little food in her stomach. Now her time in the hole seemed like a century ago. How she wished that someone had been able to come with her and Cassandra. Most of all, her father, who would have known what to do in a situation like this and also knew where the friends he'd had when he was younger lived.

We've reached a dead end, thought Caitlin, slipping into

one of her changing moods, seeing as the words came out as sharp as a knife, *aloud*. She jumped in surprise as she heard a reply.

"Pretty much," Cassandra said as her eyes fluttered open. Sleeping lightly is always the way of the Air Fairy. In the darkness of the hole and in her complete exhaustion Caitlin had never really seen Cassandra's Air Fairy form and momentarily sat on her bed, stunned and speechless by such complete natural beauty, until Cassandra laughed at her reaction. Then Caitlin smiled sheepishly and shrugged.

"Let's see if we can find some grub," grinned Cassandra, as her stomach gave an audible growl.

Both girls raced out the door and down the red carpeted hallway of the hotel. After searching on their floor for a few minutes they finally found a slightly battered vending machine.

As the wind around Cassandra grew stronger, Caitlin figured out that her friend intended to break the candy and donut filled machine. Before she got the chance, Caitlin grabbed her Air Fairy friend and snapped her back to reality, breaking the chain of magic Cassandra had been building into the air. At that moment the wind, which was awkward to have in a hotel, died off.

"Then how do you suggest we get food?" asked Cassandra, frowning as she eyed the candies and donuts with intense hunger. The most she had eaten in a while was three-quarters of a very small loaf of bread and Caitlin standing in the way wasn't helping her already irritated mood.

"Watch and learn," said Caitlin. She stepped up to the vending machine like a batter steps up to the plate and placed her hands against the cool, clear plastic, which was the only thing keeping her from getting to the food her nearly dead stomach craved.

Cassandra watched, eyes wide with wonder, as Caitlin began to sink through the plastic as though it was plastic wrap only a half an inch thick. Her hands reached forward to two large packages of donuts covered in a fine white powder. After a few seconds of struggling against the tough material, Caitlin was able to grab the donuts from their metal prison inside the vending machine as her hands broke through the now thin plastic. Coming out was another story, as Caitlin pulled as hard as she could to free her arms for at least a minute, when going in had only taken a few seconds. Her arms were only released when Cassandra gripped her waist and helped pull the arms, laden with the two slightly crushed packages of donuts, out of the hardening plastic.

Once they were out, Caitlin, who had the relieved look of someone who just escaped death upon her face and felt terribly dizzy, almost light headed, laughed to calm her pounding heart. Cassandra joined her, for her heart had also been racing as she saw her friend do something that was impossible for a vampiress to do. After all, laughter is one of the best things to do to calm down from a scary situation.

So there they stood, laughing like complete idiots, in a nearly deserted hallway. Notice the word *nearly*.

 ⁂

It should also come as no surprise to you that the other person in that corridor was a deep gray, nearly black, colored mouse. (And I assure you that I am quite sane and that this sentence will make sense if you read the next sentence!)

If you wanted to get more specific you could also say this mouse was a Changeling, who was very powerful for her age, and this creature was like no Changeling alive. Emilia—that was the Changeling's name—stood still, her mouse heart making a pleasant humming underneath her skin.

She watched the girls with amused interest, seeing what the violet-eyed female had done to the vending machine, and smiled when she heard their laughter. That was a good sign, laughter—that meant the new visitors to the hotel had a sense of humor and weren't psycho Dark Fairies.

❦❧

"How'd you do that?" asked Cassandra as the fit of laughter passed.

You see, vampires are known to have very limited magic and the only thing they can really do is the necessities, like turning invisible and straightening their teeth so their fangs can come in right. Going through a vending machine didn't really count as a necessity and Cassandra, who was a bit of a bookworm, knew what Caitlin had done with the vending machine was very much beyond her normal vampiress abilities.

"The part of Maddy's soul I have allowed me to do it," Caitlin answered.

"Did you know about Maddy's soul"—now Cassandra changed her tone from childish to serious—"before your dad told you about it?"

"I knew there was something special about me," said Caitlin, choosing her words as carefully as she spoke. "My dad said I was just different when he showed me how to pass through really thin objects. He also said that I'd find out why I was special in the future. I just had to wait for that time to come."

Cassandra nodded, looking thoughtfully off into the distance. It was true she and her father had their secrets, but then didn't everybody? But why would her father not tell her about such a special ability?

He didn't have proof, thought Cassandra suddenly. *I'd have to rely on him to tell the truth, and the truth would have seemed so ridiculous I might have thought he was a mad man. He didn't want that to happen.*

Even though Cassandra didn't necessarily agree with Caitlin's father's decision, at least now she was able to understand and cope with it.

Seems odd, she thought sadly. *Usually I'd be thinking my decisions through with my dad. Now I'm not even thinking things through, period.* She made a promise to herself to start relying, not just on instinct, but her true brain power as well. That meant no trusting strangers. Cassandra eyed Caitlin warily, ready for the possibility that she may betray her as Madore, or more correctly, Corner, had.

Caitlin was thinking the same thing as Cassandra, and all of a sudden, as the two girls searched for signs of betrayal in each others' eyes, they didn't feel like the great friends they had been five seconds ago.

෴

The watching Emilia saw this sudden change, from laughter to caution, and grinned impishly, feeling the stir of confused emotions through the very floorboards her little mouse feet clung to. A burning sensation filled her mind as the thought was erased from Emilia's brain. She wasn't even allowed to think slightly dark thoughts! The light inside her head once again tried to reason with her, telling her it wasn't nice to make fun of other people's feelings.

It also isn't nice to be bossy, but that's never stopped you, Emilia replied mentally back and in return got another burning flash of pain and a lecture on name calling. But Emilia, who had learned to tune out these frequent annoying discussions and focus herself on the real world, began to crawl forward from her hiding place in a small hole about five feet from the elevator. She had discovered this hideout when a small mouse had entered her room, number 390, through the tunnel's other side. Curiosity, which the Light had cautioned her to not satisfy, had made Emilia transform into the identical copy of the mouse. Then she had run through the hole and the tunnel, which was surprisingly clean except for the occasional mold, and crawled all the way to the other end, where she had seen the two unusual beings.

She had heard everything, though some of it had confused her, and almost believed the girls before her could be trustworthy. *Almost, but not quite,* she thought. *There's something weird about the way the violet-eyed girl smiled, like she's hiding a dark secret.* Once again a burn flashed through her mind, but Emilia hardly noticed it as she mentally apologized for having calling the girl *weird.*

Emilia had gotten to the hotel in a bit of an awkward way. Only a month ago, which seemed like a lifetime for the Changeling, she had been living peacefully with her mother on the outskirts of Earth King Territory.

It had been wonderful, she realized, only now appreciating the great life she had had with her mother and father. Like that old saying, you don't appreciate things until they're gone. She and her mother had been the village doctors in their town of Seashore, while her father had been a general in the American Army and was overseas. Everyone had come to them for injuries, some as simple and stupid as a paper cut and some as serious as a knife through the elbow. Her mother also worked as a midwife. On those calls to birth babies, Emilia would stay home while her mother went out. It was on one of these trips that everything went wrong....

☙❧

Her mother had promised Emilia she'd be home around midnight and told her to go to sleep in her room, but lock the door just in case. Then her mother, who was a Changeling like Emilia, had turned into a cheetah, in order to get to the about-to-be mother faster. Emilia, who had not yet received the light side of the soul from her mother yet, had done what she was told and entered the two-bedroom cottage, locking the door behind her.

In her true form Emilia was quite serene looking, as her mother had put it. She had dark, gentle brown eyes, smooth, slightly tanned skin, and light brown hair that fell a little ways past her shoulders. Once when Emilia was four, and her mother was telling her stories of the fairy world beyond, her mother had said Emilia didn't look like a Changeling at all, but an Earth Fairy instead. This had made Emilia so happy that she'd giggled and run around the room in excitement, trying her best to do some sort of spell. Her lack of success proved she wasn't an Earth Fairy, but Emilia was still strong in the ways of magic. At seven years old, she did her first transformation, which was odd for a Changeling, because the first transformation usually happened when the child had reached their full power at ten.

Emilia, who was twelve at the time her life changed for the worst, fell asleep quickly that night. But when she woke in the morning, her mother had not yet returned. Emilia thought nothing of it, knowing her mother's routine of getting up early in the morning to pick herbs. Usually she was back around ten o'clock. But that time came and passed, too. Now Emilia was worried, for it wasn't like her mother to leave all her patients up to Emilia's care. If some serious injury happened, Emilia wasn't sure she could handle it.

The first patient had a bloody nose, and after feeling to make sure there was no broken cartilage, she told him to hold a cloth to it until the blood stopped flowing. Another young girl had tripped, and a small stone was embedded in her knee. Emilia had given the girl three mashed-up herbs to relieve her pain, then cut the rock free with a small knife. When that was done, she cleaned and wrapped the wound and gave the girl a walking stick so she could get home more easily.

That's how it went all day, though Emilia feared some horrifying incident where a person would be nearly on their deathbed. To her great relief, that didn't happen. Instead, something just as shocking happened.

Her mother came back to the house at about ten o' clock that night. Emilia could tell it was her by the strange knock, which was their secret code to let her in when the door was locked. But when she opened the door, it wasn't just her mom standing outside the door.

Emilia had heard about Dark Fairies in stories her mother had told her. In such stories, they had sounded like fantasy creatures, but, being a Changeling, Emilia had known that they were real. Seeing one in person nearly made the twelve-year-old faint, when she spotted the distinctive black eyes and shadowlike wings. He was holding onto her mother's arm so tightly that red marks streaked her mom's snowlike skin. The man was tall and had scarily broad shoulders. He almost looked like he could squash Emilia if he took one step forward.

Emilia nearly cried out as she saw the tears on her mother's face. This was obviously not a time to ask her mom why she hadn't been home all day. Shakily her mother reached out her arms and wrapped them around Emilia's neck, squeezing her tightly and then letting go. Without saying a word her mother closed the door, left with the Dark Fairy, and Emilia was once again on her own.

But something had happened when Emilia's mother had pressed her pointer finger to the back of her daughter's neck. She had released a small light concealed within her and passed it on to her daughter.

All Emilia had felt at the time, as she stood, stunned, was a slight warmth tingling up the back of her neck all the way to where she knew the back of her brain was. At first, as she stared at the closed door in front of her, Emilia thought she had dreamed the event. She thought shock from seeing the disgustingly evil creature in her doorway had made her brain go a little fuzzy. That's when she felt the burning sensation in the back of her mind for the very first time.

"Don't call anyone ugly!" a voice said. It was the most annoying voice Emilia had heard. This voice wasn't heard by her ears, which surprised the already stunned Emilia; instead she heard it with her mind. Dizzy, Emilia listened to the first of many speeches on proper manners, taking in a voice whose owner she couldn't see but felt with her mind.

That night she fell onto her bed, trying to believe this was all a dream and when she woke up in the morning her mother would be there, with breakfast ready, and would tell her about the baby she had helped deliver. Emilia's eyelids finally closed, but she did not dream.

❧☙

It had seemed like only five seconds had passed when the sun was once again up. To Emilia's dismay, as she got down and pressed her ear to her room's door, there was no sound coming from the rest of the house.

When she opened her door the creak it made in the silence was almost deafening. She cried out when she saw the empty kitchen and her parents' empty room.

"She's probably fine," said the voice. *"Your mother is strong. Whatever they throw at her she'll be able to handle."*

"Who are you?" Emilia felt odd talking to herself. At first she didn't think the person had heard her, but then a slow, depressed response came.

"Part of a soul, the Light part, which is why I can burn you and use my brilliance against darkness when I need to. But it hurts, immensely. I feel very small and worthless without my other pieces," the voice said. Then the tone of the voice changed, as if the Light was no longer depressed. *"Your mother*

says you must gather the four other pieces. They're scattered inside four other humans in the Earth and Dark Fairy kingdoms."

"Can't you be a little more specific?" Emilia cried as the thought of the giant task her mother had left for her sank in. The voice told her four last names, two of which were common ones, Gregory and Andrews, and the other two, which were much stranger by far, Oak and Blade. But that was as far as the Light could go, though she did tell Emilia the story of Maddy and his soul, which happened two weeks before Caitlin and Cassandra were told the truth. A day ago Emilia wouldn't have believed the Light, would have thought she was going crazy and asked her mom if she could have the day off.

But Mom's not here. The shock of the thought struck deep in Emilia's soul.

So the Light and Emilia chose a random name from the bunch and decided to find the Gregory person first. The Blade person Emilia was hoping to save until last. After all, what sort of a person would have the last name of a deadly object?

It had slightly begun to snow when Emilia finished packing a small knapsack with an extra set of clothing, plenty of food, and as much cash as she could. She put on her winter coat, which was slightly small since she'd outgrown it at the end of last year. As she and the Light started their journey south, Emilia refused to look back upon the cottage she had known as her home, fearing she would cry if she did so. Instead, she focused on the road they were taking. It was made of rough stone and wound its way through a thick clump of forest, about four miles long, surrounding the back of the cottage.

Emilia shivered at the bite of the snow on her face and looked down at the path. If she would have looked up at the sky, she might have been able to avoid the incident that happened next. The snow falling was coming from dark cumulus clouds, which were forming faster than any balls of moisture you usually see in the sky. If Emilia would have been paying attention, she would have recognized, from her mother's stories, that she was in the presence of a band of Dark Fairies.

They fell out of the sky like speeding bullets; if they had been aiming at Emilia, she would surely have been dead. Luckily, just as Emilia heard the rough whistling of something cutting through the air behind her, the Dark Fairies pulled out of their dives like the professionals at flying they were. Hanging in the air about three yards from where Emilia was in all directions, forming a perfect circle in which they were all shoulder to shoulder, the Dark Fairies laughed as their prey looked up and screamed in terror. Emilia stumbled backward and fell into a newly formed pile of snow, which soaked her already chilly backside. The Dark Fairies laughed cruelly at this as their wings beat, pushing them toward their prey.

But something else was going on…something the Dark Fairies hadn't anticipated.

In Emilia's head the Light was getting stronger and stronger, until she was sure her brain was going to explode if it continued for even a minute more. Emilia writhed on the ground, her pursuer's darkness growing around her, nearly encasing her body with shadows, as the Light in her head continued to grow in brilliance. Bright white flashes began to appear in front of her eyes as she struggled not to pass out from the pain. Suddenly, like a beacon of hope in the surrounding darkness, light erupted from Emilia's body and surged toward the sky above, knocking the wind from the young Changeling's body as she was pressed down closer toward the earth she was already lying on.

Screams filled Emilia's ears, as Dark Fairies around her ran away from the light in a frenzy of panic and pain. When Emilia regained her senses, three of the Dark Fairies were already dead. Their bodies seemed to float to the ground, peaceful in death, unlike how they'd been in life. When a Dark Fairy dies, their bodies become warm, and their face and hair become golden and gentle...beautiful in death, but terrifying in life.

Emilia walked over to the deceased and bowed her head in a silent prayer.

"Nothing deserves to die." Her mother's voice echoed in Emilia's head as she finished her prayer. A tear trickled down her cheek as she thought about what the Dark Fairies might do to the person who had been her only friend and confidante through the course of her life.

Emilia shivered, only then realizing she'd been standing in wet clothing for five minutes and her thighs were more numb with each passing second. Just then Emilia felt the soft glow, which was dimmer then it had been before the burst of energy had been released, of the Light in the back of her mind, and thanked her newfound friend for saving her life. When the Light didn't answer, Emilia figured it was tired from the great amount of energy it had just used up, and decided to keep her thoughts (which seemed weird but was as easy as not thinking directly to the part of her mind the Light was in) to herself.

As the clouds began to disappear, sunlight poured down upon Emilia's face, warming up her body. But as she continued to walk, the warmth wasn't enough. Her feet began to slow down. Her backside was still drenched and felt numb. Finally, under a canopy of trees that held back the worst of the freezing droplets, Emilia transformed into a wolf.

The transformation took about the time it takes for one to blink, and Emilia used her power with the ease that comes only when you practice for hours on end. She was a strong wolf, her leg muscles thick and sturdy, unlike any wolf you could see in captivity, and her white fur was dense and smelled strongly of pine trees. Her clothes had formed to her skin, causing it to look misshapen and discolored, but only if you moved some of the dense outer covering of fur. Emilia's heart beat pounded a steady rhythm inside her chest as she pushed off nervously from the ground, towards who knew where, with such fluidity that when she landed her feet, which now had rock-hard pads and razor sharp claws, hardly made a sound and didn't break through the rapidly forming snow. She tested the form of the wolf for a while, jumping and leaping, trying out different wolves just in case the first was weaker than another animal she could think up…just in case they ran into some predator along the way. But in the end Emilia settled on her first choice, which was the best for the cold weather already forming around her.

In this form she could run swiftly, with her knapsack tied tightly around her sleek wolf body. The sunlight her enemies had run from earlier was growing overhead, lighting her way and providing her with an opportunity to find the path she had been on when she was attacked.

☙❧

A soul carrier followed silently behind the wolf, using his piece, with its own special power, to transport himself where he wanted. In the shadows he lurked, following the wolf Emilia's every move, but far enough away so she wouldn't sense him.

"Nighty night, Changeling," he whispered beneath his breath as he took a step forward from his last hiding spot behind a tree.

For the briefest instance it seemed he had completely vanished, but then, about as soon as he disappeared, he reappeared three feet in front of where Emilia, still as a wolf, was charging forward.

☙❧

Emilia would have run into the soul carrier, if he hadn't pulled out of her way at the last second. Instead, she flew forward past him and tumbled to a stop on her wolven back in a pile of snow.

She heard a sharp whistle behind her and turned swiftly. A strange boy, about a year older than herself, moved forward and whacked her sharply on the top of the head with a black staff.

Immediately Emilia felt dizzy and confused. The light in her head wasn't any better, Emilia could tell, because it was talking about the proper way to eat a banana. Slowly the world around her began to spin, as though the Earth had been twisted like a top and then let go. Darkness began to seep into Emilia's vision. Finally, after turning back into her true human form, she passed out.

༻✦༺

The boy picked her up, without the slightest bit of trouble, even though he was only a bit bigger then she was. Then, with Emilia in his arms, he took a step forward…and didn't reappear in that forest again. Instead he reappeared at the Northern New York Hotel, bought Emilia a week in a room there, and left after laying her down in the room's bed.

That's why Emilia woke to find herself in a strange room, with a room key in her hand and a note on the table from her captor saying they weren't going to harm her.

Nine

Emilia was in room 390, thinking of a plan. There wasn't enough evidence, or any at all for that matter, to help her find out who her captor and savior was. She'd been too disoriented by the cold and her experience with the Dark Fairies to get a good look at her captor's face. All she really remembered was a sharp thud to her head before everything went black.

"Grrrr!" she shrieked, picking up one of the pillows from her bed and flinging it halfway across the room in exasperation. The Light, which had grown stronger after its immense loss of energy from the other night, didn't even bother to lecture her on anger control. Instead she tried to calm Emilia by telling her everything would work out. But there was an uncertainty in the Light's voice that made Emilia feel it was not going to be so.

"If only I knew what we were up against." Emilia sighed and fell onto the hotel bed, groaning as she realized how stiff her muscles were from being a mouse for such a long period of time.

Emilia couldn't stand to be idle. As she fiddled with the remote control of the television, a wave of misery washed over her. She missed her mother terribly and wished nothing more than to see her again, alive and safe.

"*She's gone, dear, no matter how much we want her back. She's with the Dark Fairies, and only the Dark Fairy Queen herself can get her out. We'd die too if we tried to rescue her.*" It was the first time the Light had seemed solemn about something she said. Emilia knew that it killed her to do so, having heard nothing but the highest praise from the Light about how tough and strong her mother was.

A tear trickled down Emilia's cheek as the ache in her heart and the ball welling up in her throat from the wave of sadness passed. She wiped the tear away and stood up, her strength renewed, because now she knew just whom to talk to in order to get some answers about the fairy world.

"The fairy and vampires can't be staying that far away," Emilia said outloud. "It's them I'll go talk to."

The Light agreed but cautioned her about making quick decisions.

※

Outside the one window of room 390 stood a black-cloaked figure, holding a familiar black staff. He heard everything going on inside, using a spell that allowed any shadow within the room to become his ears for a short period of time. He had laughed at Emilia's struggle to figure out who he was. It was pointless, he thought. If she wanted her mother back, then she'd have to listen to him…even if he was a bad guy.

Same thing with the other two, he thought sadly, as he stood in midair, magic allowing him to sustain his balance in open space. Both Cassandra and Caitlin's fathers had been taken away, with no chance of getting them back from the Dark Fairy Queen on their own.

And just like you as well, the Darkness in his head growled menacingly.

But the boy ignored the Darkness, as though it hadn't spoken at all. He was, in fact, not even aware that the voice had spoken, having tuned his brain, ever since he was young and lived with his mother, to block out the voice completely.

※

When Caitlin and Cassandra opened their door at the hotel, they didn't expect a girl to be standing in the hallway looking for them. They didn't even realize she was looking for them until she ran straight at them down the hallway.

Startled, Cassandra nearly shot the girl's head off with one of her cannon balls of wind.

The girl shrieked, ducking from the wind, but didn't try to fight back.

"Cassandra, STOP!" Caitlin shouted over the roar of the rushing wind.

Her Air Fairy friend was in a fighting stance, her legs spaced evenly to keep her balance and her fists up and ready if it came down to hand-to-hand combat. There was a wildness in her eye, as though she was ready to kill anybody about to harm them. Caitlin realized for the first time just how powerful the Air Fairy was.

Taking a deep breath, Cassandra began to settle down, her eyes losing the crazy look about them and regaining the calm and curious look usually was on her face. Caitlin noted that her friend's breathing was perfectly calm, even though her own was rough from the near choking wind that had finally begun to stop.

"Sorry." Cassandra's apology was barely audible, even to Caitlin standing next to her.

"It's okay," said the girl clearly and calmly, like nothing had happened. Somehow she'd been able to hear what was impossible for her to hear. Obviously they were dealing with another creature of the Fairy World.

"Let's talk in our room," said Caitlin, reaching down a hand to help the girl up. "I'm Caitlin, and this is Cassandra." She pointed to the fairy.

"I'm Emilia," the girl said.

∽∼

As Caitlin opened the door to room 436, Emilia noticed that the girl's jeans were terribly dirty, and the back pocket was worn. She was awestruck by Cassandra's beauty—after all, it was the first fairy she'd ever seen. Her sight shifted, however, when a pink dog ran out the door and jumped into Cassandra's arms, barking in an annoying voice that reminded Emilia slightly of the Light inside her head.

Cassandra hugged the dog affectionately, making Emilia grin. She hadn't thought the fairy before her would go soft for a small pink puppy with silver eyes; she'd assumed Cassandra would be annoyed.

"If you don't shut Kiki up," Caitlin warned, "someone will hear her."

"Don't tell my dog to shut up!" Cassandra said, feigning hurt as she clutched Kiki to her chest. Then she spoke directly to Caitlin. "We're not going to let that nasty old vampiress treat you badly, are we, Kiki?"

The only story Emilia had ever heard about vampires was a nasty one, where most of it had been created by misinformed humans. It had been in one of her mother's fairy books and told of how vampires drank blood and killed their victims. These were untrue, though Emilia didn't know it, so she edged away from the violet-eyed Caitlin.

The vampiress saw this movement and grinned, almost wickedly. "Don't worry. I'm not going to suck—" Caitlin relaxed the muscles in her upper jaw, freeing her fangs— "YOUR BLOOD!" she yelled as her pointed teeth locked into position.

Emilia screamed and threw herself against a nearby door to a different room. It opened to reveal an old lady dressed in a bathrobe, complaining about the ruckus outside. Cassandra calmed the older lady, who wasn't able to see the actual form of the young lady she was talking to, while Caitlin pulled an unwilling Emilia into the room and closed the door almost all the way, leaving it open a fraction for Cassandra.

"Are you going to..." Emilia huddled in a corner of the room, her voice barely audible from fright.

Caitlin chuckled, turning to the one window in the room and leaning her head on the glass.

"No, I'm not going to harm you," she said, her voice dead serious to ensure the message got across. "People have feared vampires for as long as I can remember, but—" her grim attitude turned to one of mischief—"we're *usually* harmless."

Emilia nodded and stood up, though she still kept some distance between her and the vampiress, knowing it wasn't the smartest thing in the world to trust a stranger.

"What are you?"

There was such bluntness to Caitlin's question that Emilia wasn't sure how to answer it properly at first. "A Changeling," she finally whispered, her eyes looking fearfully into the unnatural violet eyes of Caitlin.

"Interesting," sighed Caitlin, once again leaning her head on the window.

There was a slight squeak of door bolts as Cassandra strode into the room, closing the vanilla-colored door behind her. The fairy looked annoyed and temperamental, like she might scream at anyone for anything.

"What's got you so upset?" Caitlin said, grinning.

Cassandra frowned, took a deep breath, and fell onto her bed. For a second nobody said anything. The awkward silence felt unbearable to the young Changeling who wanted answers desperately.

"So who are you?" Emilia asked. She wasn't sure they were going to answer, as seconds went by with still no response.

Then Cassandra, who had her eyes closed as though in deep sleep upon her bed, looked her way, as if she had just realized the Changeling was there. "Well, I'm the one more likely to kill you if you're a spy. And she—" Cassandra eyed Caitlin—"will dispose of the body once I'm done."

Emilia's legs started to quiver. Cassandra had spoken with the ease and pompous tone of an Air Fairy, making Emilia believe she would do any of the things she said. It was evident the two girls were obviously too upset with their own lives to want to help her.

I can't run, she told herself sternly. *I have to get Mom back. Fear isn't an option right now.* So Emilia held herself up strong and proudly, determined to defy the urge to flee and to ignore the screaming voice of fear in her head.

"What are your last names?" she demanded. "And it's not the time for joking." Emilia stared down Cassandra.

The Air Fairy was silent, as if searching for some hint of a lie in Emilia's tone and face. Then she nodded and stood up, as if she'd come to a decision. "My name is Cassandra Andrews. I'm an Air Fairy, in case you've never seen or heard of one before." Cassandra held a slightly silver-powdered hand out towards Emilia, and the Changeling shook it.

"I've heard of Air Fairies, but not..." She stared pointedly at Caitlin, who was still busy looking outside the window.

Cassandra grinned. "Most vampires and vampiresses are harmless, especially Caitlin Gregory."

At the mention of her full name, Caitlin turned her head from the window. "Cassandra," she said urgently, "I can feel some sort of dark presence watching us, but it's a strange, faded kind of dark presence...I can barely sense it's there!"

"That is strange." Cassandra strode over next to Caitlin at the window. Looking out she saw nothing but a street of people walking into the random shops lining the street.

But then there was the slightest tug upon her mind, like the feeling someone gets when they're being watched. The hair on the back of her neck stood up. Cassandra concentrated upon the spot until she was sure it was coming northwest from where she was standing. The Air Fairy, deep in concentration, jumped when the presence shifted positions dramatically, as it went from northeast to southwest in the blink of an eye.

"Whatever it is, it's definitely not human," sighed Cassandra, turning to Emilia. "We have to get out of here, and it would probably be best if you told us who you were before we left."

"My name is Emilia Jones, and I'm a Changeling."

"If so, you should be able to change into something for us. You understand that in times like these I can't just take your word for it."

Emilia nodded in understanding and stood tall, letting her magic seep through her body as she prepared to transform.

She decided a cute kitten form would work well enough, and concentrated upon the animal. Emilia's skin began to grow short, copper-colored hair and her entire body began to shrink. The transformation was over so fast that it was hard to describe it, but in the end Emilia was a copper kitten about the size of a very small loaf of bread. Bright green eyes had replaced Emilia's dark brown ones, and her ears had grown longer and rose to a sharp tip.

"You look so cute!" Caitlin couldn't help shrieking as she looked at the new small form Emilia had taken on. Purring happily Emilia wagged her kitty tail and turned around once. Then she stood still and transformed back into her original form.

"Impressive," whispered Cassandra, eyeing Emilia like a scientist eyes a new experiment. "You did that with such ease for your age..." She gave Emilia a questioning look.

"Twelve," responded Emilia.

"That sort of ease is nearly impossible. I've never heard of anything quite like it."

Emilia felt herself blushing as Cassandra, a powerful fairy, complimented her magic.

"But that's beside the point," Cassandra continued. "We really need to know more about you and why you knew we were in the hall."

Emilia started with her life before anything had happened, where she had lived and what she had done to help the village and ended with how she had transformed into a mouse out of curiosity. She was going to skip the part where she had gained her Light and just say her mother had told her to go south, but, before she could slip the lie into the story, she felt herself telling about the friend living in her head. Instantly she wished she hadn't, for the girls before her stared in suspicion, disbelieving eyes nearly bulging out of their heads.

"The Changeling has the Light part of the soul," whispered Caitlin, reciting what her father had told her, and Cassandra nodded, disbelief sparkling in the black pupils of her silver eyes. Emilia stared at them, unsure of how they were going to react to her ridiculous sounding story, and gave a small, almost inaudible sigh when they showed no signs of thinking she was crazy. She was, on the other hand, concerned for their sanity, because Caitlin and Cassandra were now shrieking with delight and jumping up and down like they'd just won the Nobel Prize.

"We're special," Caitlin said, grinning broadly at Emilia, stopping in mid-jump to explain, "just like you."

"Wait…" Emilia thought about the last names and laughed as she realized they were the same as the ones belonging to the people she needed to find.

Only Cassandra, once Emilia had joined them in hopping about the room in joy, stopped jumping and realized what was going on. "This isn't the time to be happy," she said solemnly, her face looking ten times paler then it usually did.

Caitlin and Emilia stopped jumping and stared at their miserable friend. "Why?" Caitlin asked, concern and fear flashing in her eyes.

Cassandra shakily pulled Kiki, who had been sleeping on the bed where her master was now sitting, to her and hugged the small creature tightly to her chest before responding. "Because we're being watched!"

Ten

"How can you know for sure?" It was the first thing that came to Emilia's mind, as she stood, dumbstruck, staring at the startled Air Fairy.

"The person we've been looking for just happens to show up when we need her, and there's a dark presence outside." Cassandra's tone was sarcastic as she gestured towards the window. "Do the math. This all can't be one big coincidence."

"Can't it?" There was a hint of plea in Caitlin's voice as she struggled to find another option to the puzzle.

"Everything can't be this simple," said Cassandra, squeezing Caitlin's shoulder reassuringly. "We'll get our parents back, but only when we understand exactly what we're dealing with and what's truly going on in the world around us."

Caitlin nodded, but the weight of the situation settled in her stomach. She hadn't thought much about her father since she'd gotten out of the hole. There hadn't been time to think when they were on the run. But now she realized how terribly she missed him.

"How do we get out of here?" Emilia's words snapped Caitlin back to reality.

"First, a practical change of costume," said Cassandra, indicating their clothing, "No offense, but a dirty vampire and a girl who looks a lot like an Earth Fairy stand out in a town of humans."

"And an Air Fairy can easily be seen from a mile away," Caitlin teased.

Cassandra laughed; she realized she was still in her natural form. A flash of silver light filled the room for a second as Cassandra resumed the form of a young hippie, awkwardly fiddling with her glasses as they resumed their place upon her face instead of her mark.

"I don't think getting dressed while someone is watching us is...," Emilia tried to point out, awkwardly searching for words to convey what she meant and shifting from foot to foot in an embarrassed fashion.

"They're too far away to be able to physically see us," Cassandra explained carefully, not sure how to describe the feeling a fairy gets when they concentrate upon the world around them and are able to detect when someone with magic is about. If only she had done that when Madore was about, she'd have been able to detect that Corner was right there in front of her. "But they can apparently sense our presence and are waiting until we come out of this building to hatch whatever trap they've set for us."

"Exactly," Caitlin agreed, though Emilia looked clueless. "Cassandra, what would we do without you?"

"Well, you'd probably still be stuck in that hole and Emilia would be trapped in this hotel alone, without any possible idea of what is going on."

Three grins spread across the faces in that room, as the teenagers realized just how true this statement was.

"Emilia, do you have any spare clothes that would fit Caitlin?"

Emilia studied Caitlin, contemplating if the few clothes she had brought would fit the five inches taller and slightly broader shouldered girl. Finally she nodded, a specific outfit in mind, and she and Caitlin walked down the hall toward her room.

When they walked in, her room was a mess, as if a tornado was staying at room 390 and not a twelve-year-old Changeling. Emilia's pack was sitting on the one chair in the room, its contents strewn about the floor. The bed's sheets and covers were tangled, and a mouse was curled up, fast asleep, on the one of the pillows. It looked like the place had been searched.

Caitlin looked at Emilia in apparent alarm. But Emilia just laughed and shook her head. "I haven't been the neatest person in the world these last few days." Emilia began to sift through the small pile of clothes shoved in one corner of the room.

"How did you fit all this stuff into that," said Caitlin, indicating the small pack and the massive piles of food, clothing, and supplies littering the room.

"My mother was in no way a fairy," Emilia began to explain.

Caitlin wasn't sure what this had to do with anything but allowed her new friend to continue.

"But simple potions weren't so hard for her to concoct. She made that bag much bigger on the inside than it looks on the outside. Its weight is as light as a feather, and none of the food in it can become spoiled. It's great for camping trips…and near-death situations," she added bitterly.

"I thought the only people who could do spells were fairies," said Caitlin as she picked up the bag and studied it closely. It looked ordinary enough, made of simple blue cloth and two hard leather straps that went over the carrier's shoulders. But when Caitlin stuck her hand inside the blue pack, she found she could in no way touch the bottom. She pushed her hand in hard, droplets of sweat forming on her brow from the strain, but the only thing she touched was open space.

"Here!" Emilia proudly held up a pair of jean capris, a pink T-shirt, and a black belt. It was true. They looked like they would fit Caitlin perfectly.

Just then something dawned on the vampiress and she cried out, "My eyes are violet! That's got to be a dead giveaway!" She buried her head in her hands. "You guys will have to go without me, while I stay here trapped in this place!"

93

Caitlin grabbed a pillow from the bed and chucked it halfway across the room. There was no way she was going to be trapped somewhere again. Not after the hole had instilled a fear of being caged within her. Being locked up again so soon, without anyone to help her this time, would surely drive her mad.

"Calm down, calm down," Emilia said. "I'm sure Cassandra will think up a solution!"

Those words silenced the sobbing vampiress. Her new Air Fairy friend had already thought up plans to get them closer to having Maddy's full soul, so it was stupid to worry about something as simple as eye color. Caitlin took a deep breath, wiped the tears stinging her eyes, and stood with the pile of clothes laden in her arms.

☙❦

While Caitlin dressed in Emilia's room, Emilia returned to room 436. When she walked in, using Caitlin's card to unlock the door, Cassandra was pacing the length of the room. Her brows were furrowed in intense concentration and her hands were shoved deep into her jean pockets. It was almost funny to see an Air Fairy looking that way…so human.

When Emilia entered the room, Cassandra stopped pacing and turned to the Changeling.

"Caitlin is worried about her eye color," Emilia said, dreading that Cassandra would say there was nothing she could do, "It's a dead giveaway if our stalker sees violet eyes in a crowd of humans."

"A simple illusion spell will do the trick then."

Emilia breathed a sigh of relief.

"She actually may be the safest of us when she walks out."

Emilia's eyebrows raised in question.

"She'll be touched by fairy magic, but only slightly, making her look like a human we're simply using as bait," Cassandra explained.

"What about us, then?"

It was the question Cassandra couldn't fully answer.

Emilia saw this change in attitude, as Cassandra's eyes darkened from their light sea green color to a deep emerald any time she wasn't totally honest, and wondered if she could really trust these new friends of hers.

"You'll be touched by magic too," said Cassandra slowly, "along with any other human in the lobby that we can get to go out the door. I'll make sure of that."

"And what about you?"

Cassandra turned away from Emilia and shook her head, miserably. "Of all three of us it's me that whoever is out there can sense so easily. If I leave, they'll pick me out like a large diamond in a pile of coal!"

If Emilia got nervous when Caitlin got upset, then she was terrified when Cassandra started to lose control. The air in the room started to swirl in different directions, forcing Emilia to gasp for the tiniest amounts of oxygen. She struggled to get closer to the floor, where it was easier to breathe.

Tears splashed down Cassandra's front, the bright silver droplets disappearing as soon as they hit cloth. Emilia watched, trying to keep her breath even, as the unnatural sight of a human girl crying silver tears unfolded before her. Cassandra struggled to procure some small object from the front pocket of her jean coat. When she found what she was looking for, she pulled out a small glass vial about the size of your pinky finger. The Air Fairy held the vial to her eyes and began to cry into it, collecting the silver fluid while the air around her began to settle back into its normal position.

Emilia staggered as she pulled herself up from the floor. Her ribcage stung where she had flung herself down on the carpet and her lungs were still cramped from lack of oxygen.

She took slow, hard breaths, trying to relax her burning muscles, while she watched the fairy collect her own tears.

"What…are…you…doing?" she managed to wheeze out.

Cassandra collected the last few tears and put the stopper in the top of the small vial. The liquid inside the glass oozed and swirled. Emilia felt an immense power radiating from it.

"There are magical properties in fairy tears," Cassandra answered at last, grinning awkwardly as she pocketed the bottle. "And I think I just found my ticket out of here."

Emilia didn't ask Cassandra what she meant by this, because at that moment someone began knocking on the door. The Changeling's first reaction was to try to get out of there by any means possible, afraid whoever was knocking wasn't a friend. This was a bit absurd, seeing as an enemy would doubtlessly not give them the advantage of knowing he/she was right outside their room.

Cassandra laughed. "Relax. It's just Caitlin. She doesn't have her room key. You used it to get in—remember?"

Emilia looked down at her hand and laughed. She was actually holding the little piece of plastic.

Cassandra walked over and checked the peephole just in case. It was Caitlin. When she walked in the door, the other girls stared. Caitlin looked ten times healthier then Cassandra had ever seen her. The girl's dark blonde hair was pulled up into a neat bun, obviously after a thorough brushing. Her face was slightly pink. Emilia had let her borrow a few napkins and a bottle of water to clean away some of the dirt, revealing skin that shone with an unhealthy white hue, a sign of the fact that she hadn't been in sunlight for a month.

Emilia had been a genius where the clothes were concerned. The pink shirt was long and slightly form-fitting, while the black belt went around the shirt, resting lightly on the girl's hips, instead of on the jean capris. It made Caitlin look almost…

Normal. A human teenager in the midst of two inhuman-looking females.

"Who are you, and what has a normal human like yourself done with our vampiress friend Caitlin?" Cassandra joked.

Caitlin hit at Cassandra playfully, then her attitude changed swiftly. "What about my eyes?"

Cassandra gave her a reassuring look. "Leave that to me. There's a simple Latin spell that should fix both you and Emilia so that you look completely different from your true forms."

"You don't have to bother with me," the Changeling said impishly. "I can take care of myself." In a split second a tall blonde woman had taken the spot where Emilia had been standing. Her thin, ratty looking hair fell about an inch from her earlobe, she had a hooked nose, and giant freckles covered the majority of her face. Her skin was starting to wrinkle, making her look like she was in her forties, but at the same time she appeared to be in her twenties. It was obvious from the blue high heels and matching suit that she was a businesswoman, though not a very attractive one.

A confusion of a face, Caitlin thought, *like going through puberty as an adult.*

"This lady came to collect taxes from our house, but since we built our house on land not owned by the government, and we never bought our goods from government facilities, except for certain things from the town, she stormed away empty handed." Emilia, still in the form of the business woman, grinned at the thought of the old memory. It had only been a year ago, but now it felt like a lifetime away.

"I still can't believe any of this is real," Emilia said. "It feels like I'm just in a really bad dream."

"Then let's hope this nightmare ends soon," whispered Cassandra solemnly. "You and Caitlin will go downstairs with all of your stuff packed, and I'll meet you there."

"Why don't you come with us?" Caitlin's eyes flashed with

distrust for a minute before she remembered she had nothing to lose if Cassandra wasn't telling the truth.

"I need to focus my power for a minute," Cassandra said. "I'm going to need a lot of energy for the plan ahead. Besides, I have to make sure Kiki is ready to go!"

At the mention of her name the little pink dog jumped eagerly into her master's awaiting arms, snuggling up against the young girl until she was in a comfortable position.

Caitlin and Emilia nodded obediently, took one of the room keys, and left. Cassandra was sure she saw Emilia roll her eyes at Kiki when the Changeling thought she wasn't looking, but perhaps that was just her imagination.

<hr />

Caitlin and Emilia walked down the hallway swiftly, their hearts racing as they realized just what they were about to do. Whoever was outside was after them, and they had no clue as to what they were up against.

As soon as they entered room 390 both girls began stuffing things into the small pack on the chair. Caitlin was glad, as she picked up odd herbs and strange bottles filled with awkward colored fluids, that she didn't have to work with this sort of stuff on a daily basis, because it was all very confusing.

Soon there was nothing left in the room but the furniture and Emilia now held a small, light pack that was still as big as it had been five minutes ago. Both girls gave the room a final glance, hoping they hadn't forgotten anything important and walked out of the room to meet Cassandra.

<hr />

Cassandra was standing next to the elevator, with Kiki at her heels, when the other two girls caught up with her. She was rapidly punching the elevator button, and obviously it wasn't working.

Cassandra was upset beyond a normal human's reaction. "We're trapped!" she shrieked, throwing herself at the elevator door, which still outwardly refused to move a fraction of an inch.

"Just relax and take the stairs," groaned Caitlin, walking to the opposite side of the hall where the door for the stairs was. She gripped the handle and pulled, but the door didn't budge an inch. Caitlin pulled again, this time using all of her strength against the door, and still it did not move.

"Do you think I wouldn't have already tried that?" shrieked Cassandra as she launched two of her air cannon balls at the door. There was a resounding thud, which caused Kiki to bark in surprise as the air hit its mark, but the door remained firmly in place.

"What about the windows in our room?"

But before Caitlin could get a reply, she was stunned speechless by a familiar face walking down the hall towards them, blocking the way to their rooms. Kiki growled, a low-throated growl that Cassandra was sure couldn't have come from something as sweet and adorable as Kiki.

"We ARE trapped," whispered a terrified Emilia as she fell against a nearby wall into a sitting position on the floor, safely positioned behind Cassandra, staring down the hall at the approaching figure.

"Basically," the cold voice said, making the girls shiver.

Cassandra glared down the hallway in utter disgust as her worse nightmare stared back at her.

With a wicked grin broadening on his face with every step, Corner was walking down the hall toward them.

The girls had no way to escape.

Eleven

Cassandra and Caitlin's first instinct was to attack Corner with everything they had, and Emilia's first instinct was to scream, her last encounter with Dark Fairies still fresh in her memory. The boy walking down the hallway definitely had a Dark Fairy look about him, even though he wasn't in his true fairy form.

But none of them got the chance, because Corner held his hands up, like a gesture of peace and innocence, and stood halfway down the hall from the three stunned girls. Only Cassandra knew that Corner was too far away to do any real damaging magic (unless he had been an Air Fairy, because their wind blasts could travel great distances), so she relaxed her magic a little. But she still held her mind concentrated on her power, in case anything else unexpected happened.

Corner's clothes, eyes, and hair were still their usual black, except for his jeans and white sneakers. But his usually greasy hair was combed and, to Cassandra's amazement, he seemed to have taken a shower since the last time she had seen him. Since he wasn't in his fairy form, his wings were nowhere to be found, and it was odd seeing him without those extra limbs.

"I'm not here to harm anyone," he said in a voice that held...

Warmth. Both Cassandra and Caitlin glanced at each other in surprise, not sure of who this person was before them. He had the features and build of Corner, but the gentleness surely proved it wasn't him.

"Who are you?" Cassandra managed to ask.

Corner chuckled before answering, "I'm not so sure myself, but I think I'm both a light and a Dark Fairy."

Cassandra was quite sure she hadn't heard Corner correctly, but when the two girls beside her looked at her questioningly, she knew she had to say something. "What?" She tried to hide her confusion with a poker player-like face.

A flash of golden light filled the hallway, momentarily blinding its female occupants. When they finally regained their vision, white flashes played across their sight for a few minutes, causing them to feel slightly dizzy.

Standing before them was a sight that turned all three girls momentarily speechless…even Cassandra, who was used to the transformations of her people. Corner no longer looked like himself, or like the dark-winged beast he was known to become. In fact, this version of Corner was quite the opposite of dark. His new wings, which sprouted brilliantly outward, looked like bright, shooting lights that reached toward the sky with a gentle elegance and beauty. The four new limbs also might be described as giant crystals, rising from the young man's back and then coming to a sharp tip at the part closest to the sky. In many ways the wings were very much like Cassandra's—butterfly-like and amazing in a way no normal human will ever be able to comprehend.

Golden eyes, slightly dimmer then the usual brilliance of an ordinary Light Fairy, stared at the girls with amusement. Corner's hair was no longer dark, but a shiny blonde—almost golden, but not quite—color. Cassandra also noted that his clothes were almost identical to her fairy clothing, except they were gold, not silver, and Corner's skin was no longer a pale white but a healthy tan color, though still not the lustrous gold color normal Light Fairies were known for.

His mark was a lot more subtle then Cassandra's—just a gold, crescent-shaped moon painted on his left cheek that seemed to melt into his tan skin.

"But you changed into a Dark Fairy! You can't change into a Light Fairy if you're a Dark Fairy—it's not physically and scientifically possible. The magic in your blood just doesn't allow it!" Cassandra cried, confused and stunned beyond her wildest dreams. After all, she had spent years researching stuff like this. Now, for the first time, she knew how humans felt when they found that fairies were indeed real.

Up to this point, Cassandra had been able to see logic in most things...and that proved she wasn't going crazy. Now she sank against a nearby wall, with formulas and scientific knowledge playing across her brain, searching for an answer that would tell her she wasn't suddenly going delusional.

"The magic in my body can usually be tricked into thinking I'm a Dark Fairy, because of the piece of the soul I carry," Corner said.

Caitlin could suddenly be abducted by aliens and not be any more surprised than she was at this moment. The odds of Corner being a fairy, knowing about the soul, and carrying the dark part of the soul, were a million to one.

"What if it's just an illusion spell? Like the one you were about to put on Caitlin to change her eye color?" Emilia asked.

"You can't give the illusion of being a fairy," Cassandra explained. "It's either something you are—or you aren't." Cassandra stared Corner down, trying to find a hint of a lie within his new golden eyes. There was only a faintly amused expression, like he was enjoying their apparent fear.

At least that's one sign that he's still the sick, psycho Dark Fairy we all know he is, Cassandra thought. But as these thoughts passed through her head in a blur, she wasn't sure that was necessarily so. When Corner smiled, it was with a warmth and happiness that could be seen on even an ordinary boy's face. His eyes were gentle, almost honest. How could someone with such kind features possibly be the evil person she was used to seeing in nightmares?

He fooled you before, she told herself sternly, and held onto the notion that he could still betray her, or that anyone in that hall, for that matter, could turn on her.

"Let me explain," Corner said. "Once there was a man named Maddy…"

Cassandra held up her hand to stop him. "I think most of us have heard this story." She questioned Emilia with her gaze, and Emilia nodded with a shy smile.

"The Light in my head told me!" Emila said. Even though she sounded slightly insane when she said this, nobody questioned her.

☙❧

Funny, Emilia thought to herself and the Light in her head, *this all feels so unreal. Like some strange parallel universe where everything is upside down.*

"Well, believe it, hon," said the Light, *"because you're right in the middle of this fantasyland."*

There was an edge to the Light's voice that Emilia had never heard before, but she decided it would be better not to comment on it.

"So—" Cassandra's voice brought Emilia back to the present—"you're saying you're the fourth soul piece holder, and we're supposed to just go along with this and believe you? If you're a good guy, then why'd you try to kill me?"

She was talking, Emilia knew from the story Cassandra had told her, about the time Corner had lifted her up into the air with magic and violently tossed her about, nearly splitting her neck in two.

"But I didn't kill you, did I?" he pointed out, another devious grin playing across his face.

Cassandra looked troubled. Clearly she wasn't dead, so he had a point.

But Caitlin beat her to the punch and asked the obvious question: "If you knew it was us holding the soul pieces all along, then why didn't you just kill us? Or kill everyone in the town who had magic? You have to be a good guy, or by now we would have been dead."

"Yes, because I, unlike my Dark Fairy comrades whom you had the pleasure of meeting that night—" sarcasm was heavily laden in his voice—"can't kill. The Light Fairy part of my magic keeps me from doing so. It sickens me to see death, so, naturally, I disagree with everything the Dark Queen does." His voice reminded Emilia of a young British gentleman—articulate, composed, and detailed enough to be sure the point got across.

Emilia recalled something she'd asked Caitlin, right before she gave her the clothes she'd picked out for her. "Have you encountered a Dark Fairy before?" she'd asked, thinking about her own previous encounter with a group of the fiendish creatures.

"Once. A Dark Fairy named Corner. He was the most selfish, evil, absurdly cruel person I know I will ever meet in my life." Caitlin's voice had been strangled by such rage that Emilia knew, with certainty, that the next time Caitlin saw this Corner person, the vampiress would tear him to shreds.

So now Emilia was puzzled. She saw nothing evil about the Light Fairy in front of her. Sure, he wasn't as bright as the beautiful golden-colored Light Fairies in her mother's books, but he had gentle eyes, and a wide smile replacing his evil grin.

He's proud of himself, she noted. *Proud that he's not a Dark Fairy, but something good and kind instead.*

When Corner's gaze turned from Cassandra to Emilia, the young Changeling realized she was staring. She turned her eyes, feeling the heat of an embarrassed flush on her cheeks. Yet, given the current situation, she couldn't help but stare. She was the only one with practically no clue what was going on and no real experience with magic (other than her own ability of transformation). She had never seen Corner before but had been told he was one of the worst Dark Fairies alive. In addition, he was a year younger than the rest of the group in the hallway.

༄༅

"I'm...," Corner began in a tone as if he was about to quote from something.

Cassandra interrupted. "If you're about to quote from *Beowulf*, or something like it, then just save your breath, because I tried reading that story and only understood about a quarter of the things they were saying,"

Even though the situation they were in was so serious it could mean life or death, Cassandra sounded so much like a young teenager that the vampiress couldn't help but laugh. And from the way Corner glowered at the Air Fairy Caitlin guessed that Cassandra had read what he was about to do perfectly.

"Fine," he said, "but you can be sure of one thing: I've been the only thing standing between you and death lately, so you should be a bit more trusting."

Questions surged to the girls' lips and they looked at each other, a silent decision as to who would go first.

"How in the world can you be two fairies at once?" Cassandra asked.

He shrugged. "Simple. As I've just told you, the piece of Maddy's soul tricks the magic in me to think I'm a Dark Fairy, it lessens the power I possess as a Light Fairy, but it's efficient enough that the dark queen can't see me for what I really am. I'd be killed on sight if the truth got out."

"So you're a spy. But for whom do you spy?" Emilia asked, her head cocked as she considered Corner more closely.

"*My* queen, who is in no way the foul Dark Fairy I'm pretending to serve, is otherwise known as the Queen of Light.

She sent me here when I traveled to Australia after my mother died in Earth Fairy Territory. She requested that I use my soul piece to trick the Dark Queen into trusting me, ensuring that it would be simple if I ever needed to free someone from one of the Dark Fairy prisons on the lowest floor of Castle Storm, the Dark Queen's personal headquarters. My queen also requested that I free Madore's soul, free the Dark Queen of the curse embedded into her very being, and find someone better suited to become the new queen. And, I might add, that sounded a lot simpler than it actually is."

"So you purposefully meant for us to leave that foul dark hole that *you* trapped us in? Wouldn't it have just been easier to find us, tell us what's going on, and tell the Dark Queen we're dead?" Caitlin's tone was layered with sarcasm, earning her a nasty glare from Corner.

"It's not quite that simple. The Dark Queen trusts me about as much as she can trust anyone. She still thinks I may stab her in the back, so she has a bunch of her Dark Fairies follow me wherever I go, all of whom hate me and are willing to report any crimes I commit against the queen. So, in other words, no, I couldn't have just simply told her you were dead, unless I wanted to end up dead myself."

"Wait...I'm confused." Emilia was looking at the scene playing out in front of her with a clueless expression. "So you're Corner—" she pointed toward the Light/Dark Fairy and he nodded—"and your last name is..."

"Blade," he answered a little too quickly.

Ah, thought Caitlin as she eyed the way Corner seemed to look over Emilia, *I think I smell two people crushing in the air. Teenage hormones....*

"And you're one of us?"

"Yes, except for the fact that I'm not a female," he pointed out with a small chuckle.

"Right. And you were the one that brought me here?"

Corner simply nodded.

"Then why couldn't you have just brought them—" she gestured toward Caitlin and Cassandra—"here like you did me?"

"Because, as I just pointed out, I was being followed."

"But I'm not really sure that answers the question!" Emilia insisted.

So there was a loophole in Corner's story. Could he be lying to them?

Twelve

"I had"—Corner stared at the floor and then looked up again before continuing—"orders to kill three girls. One was an Air Fairy living in the southern part of New York; another was to kill whoever had the soul in that town Caitlin lived in."

"The town's got a name you know!"

Corner ignored Caitlin's rude interruption and waited for Emilia to reply.

"And you were afraid we wouldn't trust you if you told us the truth." Emilia had seen right through Corner's pretense. She was an expert at things like this, being a master of disguise herself.

"It's a Dark Fairy's nature to play with people they are supposed to murder. It would only be natural if I told you that you'd think that's exactly what I'm doing with you. But I'm a Light Fairy. The part of the soul I have just makes it seem like I'm a Dark Fairy, but I don't do the things a Dark Fairy does."

"So we'd have to be relying on your word, and you can see why that wouldn't be easy, given the state of things?"

Corner nodded and Cassandra pondered this for a minute. "But you said the soul piece weakens your abilities as a Light Fairy and a Dark Fairy, so hypothetically speaking…"

"You would be able to beat me in a fight." Corner had to clench his teeth together and stare at the floor with a steely expression in order to get this sentence out.

Cassandra smiled, slightly devilishly, as Corner had a hard time admitting she was stronger, which is always a hard thing for a fairy to do.

The Changeling and vampiress in the hallway had no clue how important this statement was and the meaning of it. One fairy telling another fairy that they were weaker was an ultimate sign of trust, even for Dark Fairies, who rarely abided to the fairy laws put down by the first fairies known to exist. Corner had basically pledged that he would in no way hurt Cassandra or anyone close to her.

"That's good enough for me." She glanced questioningly towards Caitlin and Emilia, who stared at her with an unfathomable look.

"What?" asked Emilia.

"That's it! After everything we've been through, you're just going to trust him because he *says* you can beat him?!" There was a note of hysteria in Caitlin's voice. "I say there's no way we go *anywhere* with this rat-faced scoundrel." Those last words weren't necessarily true, for, in his new Light Fairy form, Corner didn't look anything like a rat, but more like a young teenage lion, just beginning to find his way into manhood.

"Yeah, Cassandra, I don't like the sounds of this," Emilia added. "I just met you two, so trusting someone else so quickly…"

"Would not be a smart thing to do on your part, I know, but he gave his fairy word. A vampiress," Cassandra added, as Caitlin looked daggers at her, "wouldn't understand." The words were cold enough to give Emilia goosebumps and to silence her.

"Well, I guess he's not a good fairy," Caitlin mocked cruelly, repeating what Cassandra had said when Corner had lifted her from the hole when she had been sleeping, violating one of the many fairy rules.

"There was a loop hole…he didn't necessarily attack me," Cassandra insisted.

"I still don't trust him," Caitlin fired back.

Cassandra rolled her eyes and shook her head but did not say anything more to defend Corner. "Be that as it may, I say we take a vote." Cassandra glared at Caitlin, daring the vampiress to defy her.

"As long as *he* isn't one of the voters." Caitlin made a show of saying *he* as though Corner weren't standing in the room with them.

"All in favor of following Corner?" Cassandra asked to the group at large. Both she and Emilia raised their hands in the air, while Caitlin glowered at them silently.

"I'm no politician, but I think you just got outvoted," Cassandra said, turning away from the infuriated vampiress to Corner. "Now what exactly are we going to do?"

"How does infiltrating Castle Storm sound?"

ಊಬ

The plan was simple enough, possibly a little too simple. All of them would go in, Corner in his Dark Fairy form, Emilia disguised as a mouse in the one pocket of his tunic, and Caitlin and Cassandra would be in chains, acting as Corner's prisoners. When asked by the fairy guards at the front gate where they were going, Corner would say fairy dungeon 4, one of the higher security prisons.

It was here that the last soul holder was being held. Torture and threats had forced him to say where the other soul holders, except Corner, whose position he had lied about, were. It was the gift his soul piece gave him, the ability to know where anyone on the world was at any given point of time.

The young man had told Corner personally where the other three soul holders were hidden, and also that Corner shouldn't give himself away by freeing him, until he had the other three soul pieces. Corner promised to return for the boy, whose name was Hunter, as soon as he possibly could.

"So that's how they knew one of the soul holders was in my town!" Caitlin had given up trying to convince Cassandra that Corner wasn't one to put faith in, so now she was giving the cold shoulder to her Air Fairy friend.

"Exactly," Corner said, standing over the little table in Emilia's room, edging slightly closer to where Emilia was sitting on his right side. All four of them had gone back to Emilia's room to formulate a way to break into the Castle Storm. This didn't seem remotely possible, given the fact that only three other known fairies had ever been able to get into the castle uninvited, and all three of them were now dead.

"There's a difference, though, between us and them," Corner had pointed out enthusiastically when they had been discussing the matter.

"And what would that be?" said Caitlin, her tone icy.

"Each of the three times the fairies went in alone, without help from inside the castle. And given the new amount of prisoners in the castle…"

"Two more creatures aren't going to be very noticeable," Cassandra finished for him and Corner nodded his approval. He seemed to admire the way Cassandra's brain worked out puzzles like she had been in these situations all her life, and Emilia saw this at once. For a second she almost felt jealous, but a sharp flash of pain and another scolding on unjust thoughts stopped that feeling abruptly.

"I have a question!" Caitlin announced and looked Corner in the eye to make sure he was completely honest when he gave his response. "Where are the Dark Fairies that Queen Kendra sent with you, now?"

"In a clearing twenty miles away. They saw me go into my tent to sleep today and then went to their own tents." Corner smiled. "Little do they know I don't have as much trouble walking around in the sunlight as they do."

"Dark Fairies sleep during the day?" Emilia asked, and he

nodded politely.

"Light hurts us, so we can't walk around when the sun's out without making clouds, and that saps us of most of our magic." After explaining that to Emilia, Corner turned back to Caitlin to see if she would like to continue. And indeed she did.

"They didn't hear you leave?"

"No, I didn't leave in the normal way a human would. I—" he met the three girls' eyes with an intense gaze—"I'll show you how I left."

Corner stood up from where he had been sitting between Emilia and Cassandra on the bed. Caitlin had refused to be anywhere near Corner, so she had grabbed the one chair in the room and positioned it on the opposite side of the table. Corner vaulted over the bed, so that he was now standing in a wide space of the room that was empty.

The Light Fairy, still in his normal form, leaned back on the heel of his right sandal, which was slightly thick-soled in the back to allow the wearer to spin, just like Cassandra's. And that was exactly what Corner did, as he moved with the grace fairies were known for and spun three times on his right leg while he held the other four inches off the ground. It was happened so quickly Emilia was sure that if she had blinked, she would have missed it.

Halfway through Corner's fourth spin it was like the world went into slow motion. Corner was still turning, about halfway through his last spin, when it was, for a fraction of a second, like he didn't exist. The Dark/Light Fairy was nowhere in the room or in existence, for that matter. Another second later he was back, only this time he was on the opposite side of the room, standing behind where Caitlin had situated her chair, and he had finished his fourth spin.

No one in the room reacted at first. Corner watched the three girls, waiting for them to say something or move, while the girls stood perfectly still, an incomprehensible look in their eyes. Finally, as was to be expected by her status in the group she was now leader of, Cassandra spoke.

"That was...*unexpected.*" It was the best word she could think of to describe Corner's hocus-pocus act, since the magic in front of her was like nothing she had ever dealt with before, kind of like how she had felt when Corner turned out to be a Light and Dark Fairy. Her whole life she had studied the future advancements fairies would make in their magic, things that included becoming two fairies at once, but those improvements were centuries off in the distance, which, in fairy years, wasn't quite so long as it may seem to a human.

"Yeah, kind of like what I can do! Only in a different form..." Corner's gaze lingered on Caitlin's face questioningly as she spoke and she explained her ability to pass through thin objects.

"Only his ability is magnified by the fact that he has strong fairy blood flowing through his veins." Cassandra stood up and paced the room, lost in thought.

"Okay, back on topic. How do we get to the queen after we have this dude we need to get?" Emilia said, her eyes glued on Corner.

He noticed and grinned at her, causing her to blush and stare down nervously at the floor. "Simple," he said and reached over to squeeze the Changeling's arm playfully.

<hr>

It looked like a giant, dark chocolate cake. That description may not be used often to describe castles, but it was what Cassandra thought as she looked upon the Castle Storm for the first time.

The castle was enormous, there was no doubt about it, and it seemed to be a town in itself, with Dark Fairies running amuck in every direction on all sorts of errands. The young Air Fairy, used to seeing strong, tall male Dark Fairies, was amazed by the diversity you could see in the fairy faces around her. Status didn't seem to be based on skin color, gender, or beauty, but on magical promise certain fairies seemed to show. This was strange, seeing as Dark Fairies were very egotistical and preferred to have those who were beautiful and comely to be the first anyone saw upon entering one of their domains. Obviously Queen Kendra was running things a little differently than a normal Dark Fairy monarch would.

The first fairy Cassandra saw upon entering the castle was anything but beautiful. A Dark Fairy, short and stocky, with a piglike face that would have put any boar to shame, greeted them at the giant arched entrance with a sour look. He nodded toward Cassandra and Caitlin, who were wrapped in the black cloaks prisoners wore and had chains wrapped securely around their hands and feet, binding the two girls together and making walking nearly impossible. Corner nodded grimly and with the same sour expression, like he had smelled something foul. (Kiki had been forced to stay back at the hotel for fear that she would bark and risk revealing that Caitlin and Cassandra weren't prisoners.)

The young Dark/Light Fairy was no longer in his Light Fairy form, but in his Dark Fairy one. It was eerie, seeing him so pale, so unlike how he had been in the hallway just yesterday, when he had seemed so energetic, so much more like a normal teenager. Now he looked like an empty shell, a mere shadow of the young man the girls were, by now, used to.

The great arched entrance the disguised soul carriers were passing through was located in the north, built of blackened stone, and connected to a wall that extended the entire length of the castle. There were three other entranceways facing the south, east, and west part of the castle.

Inside the great stone walls the fairies weren't quite as busy. Only a few servants sold goods, such as magical ingredients, in the large courtyard. It was lined with potted plants unlike anything in the human world. Some snapped out at you as you walked by; others grew at such a quick rate that they were overflowing their pots; and one, Caitlin was sure, even barked at her as she passed. One thick, barbed-wire-like plant, reached forward and tried to snatch Emilia, who was disguised as a mouse, from Corner's front shirt pocket. The young girl squealed and tried to shove herself further into Corner's pocket, but the Dark Fairy grabbed the vine, which lashed out wildly in his grip, and snapped it cleanly in two with the back of its palm. Two more vines stretched from the plant and caught the broken one, dragging it back to the core of the plant as though to nurse it back to health.

"Hey!" a servant dressed in black rags called, running up behind Corner. He was tall, gangly, and had the eyes of a large hawk. The servant was so agitated that every time he spoke spittle flew from his mouth and a vein in his left temple bulged alarmingly.

Cassandra had to bite down on her lip until it bled to keep from laughing aloud.

"You hurt one of the queen's plants, so you have to do hard labor for a month to make up for it!" the servant growled menacingly, his eyes glued on Corner.

"You yell at the queen's assistant, and he's liable to kill you," Corner answered coolly.

The servant stared in horror at the displeasure the queen would feel if she learned he had been disrespectful to one of her most important workers. His family would not live long if the queen heard of his insolent behavior.

"I'm sorry, sir, forgive me!" The servant bowed so low that his nose nearly touched the ground and Corner laughed—a cruel, high-pitched, soul-less laugh, like the one he had given Cassandra when she hadn't realized he was Madore.

"I don't forgive, I forget, you worthless piece of trash!" One of Corner's black penny loafers flew upward, hitting the slave squarely on the knees. The slave's legs flew out from underneath him, and he fell with a resounding thud to the ground and didn't move. Cassandra knew the slave wasn't dead, though, because he retained his Dark Fairy state and didn't change into the gorgeous form Dark Fairies obtained when they were dead. He had merely hit his head on the stone pathway and was unconscious.

"We better be long gone by the time he wakes up," Corner said, ushering them forward as he did so.

As soon as Caitlin and Cassandra, still bound together by iron chains, tried to move faster, they fell, hard, in a pile of chains and limbs, to the ground. A slave passing by looked on curiously, and Corner was forced to act the role of an evil fairy captor. He mumbled something incoherent about the stupidity of vampires and Air Fairies, turned to the two creatures trying to disentangle themselves from each other, grabbed both of them by the collar of their black prisoner robes, and began dragging them roughly down the stone pathway toward a black door inlaid in the western stone wall of the castle's border. This door, which Corner opened by placing his palm on the smooth surface a certain way and pushing, led to a spiral staircase of a turret that extended up and beyond the border of the great stone wall. Here he let the two girls go for enough time for them to get back on their feet.

Cassandra was amazed that she had missed this towerlike structure when they had been traveling along the western side of the castle. She was sure she hadn't seen anything of the sort, but shrugged, knowing the answers to the million questions burning within her would be answered for her soon enough.

The cool, smooth stone echoed eerily every time one of the soul holders took a step upward on the winding staircase, and Caitlin shivered involuntarily. Torches, like ones you see in those old medieval movies, were hooked to the wall with iron pegs every five feet, their glow casting shadows against the walls, which were closely pressed together so you could only move forward. Walking forward, in such a dreary place, felt like monotonous work. After a while Cassandra wasn't sure if it was minutes or hours that had passed.

Finally the tunnel of the staircase opened up onto a large, circular room about half the size of a football field. The first thirty yards were reserved for the guards, tables for the guards to eat and play poker on, and torture weapons to force the prisoners to give information about other fairy countries. Caitlin shuddered as she saw a particularly nasty set of spike-tipped whips hooked on pegs on a wall to her right.

The last twenty yards was barred off, like the kind of room you see in old western movies, and about thirty prisoners were crammed inside it.

"This place is disgusting," Cassandra whispered close to Corner's ear so he was the only person who could hear her.

He didn't answer, just kept his face as cold and hard as marble. His dark eyes were fixed on the two guards—one of whom was sleeping in a chair, the other who was talking to a female prisoner about forty years old. The first guard was snoring so loudly, so deep in sleep, that he didn't notice the new arrivals. Guard two, on the other hand, did.

When he saw Corner, the first thing he did was stare and his mouth moved, though no words came out. Like all the other Dark Fairies that roamed the castle, the two guards were unmistakably dirty. Their features were distorted by helmets, and they also wore chain mail, plate bodies, gauntlets, and belts with sheaths for their huge, two-handed, medieval swords that were at least four feet long and one foot thick.

After Guard Two pulled himself together, he stood up, kicked the other guard, who woke with a start, and both of them bowed before Corner.

"Sir, what are the Queen's orders for what should be done with these prisoners?" The second guard spoke in rough, nasally tones, like someone with a seriously bad cold.

"I'm taking over your shifts for a few days; the queen wants all of her men down at the battle arena for a victory celebration that will take place at this time tomorrow. The prisoners of this tower are so important I decided I'd better watch them just in case."

The two guards nodded dutifully and marched out, eyeing the two new prisoners cautiously as they went. As soon as they were far enough away that Cassandra could no longer feel their presence by magic, she nodded—the signal to reveal themselves to the prisoners.

Swish!

Wind swirled around the room, whistling through the bars of the cage and shaking the chains of various torture instruments. Both Cassandra and Caitlin felt it tug at their bodies, yanking the leather cords that held their prisoner cloaks on apart and breaking the chains around their hands and ankles to pieces. Then the rushing air caught the costumes when they were about to float to the ground and flung them, with a resounding crash of metal on metal, to the opposite side of the room, where they slammed into a strange iron torture device, splitting it cleanly in two.

Underneath the costumes Caitlin was wearing the same outfit she'd had on in the hotel, and Cassandra was in her fairy form.

Emilia, still a mouse, jumped out of Corner's pocket and was human again before she hit the floor.

Most of the prisoners just stared, shocked.

But one started laughing.

He was close enough to where the four soul carriers were standing that Cassandra could see his face and figure clearly through the bars that kept him from reaching the four people who were so much like him.

And the sight of that young child nearly made Cassandra

cry. His face was bruised and scraped, though not nearly as much as some of the adults around him. He couldn't have been more than six years old. His face still held some of its baby roundness, but his body was so malnourished he could no longer move properly. The laugh that echoed from his throat was a haunted, defeated sound, an eerie form of mock joy coming from one so young. Another large difference between him and the four Caucasians who were not behind bars, was that his skin was the color of chocolate, and his eyes were such a bright green that Emilia was sure this had to be Hunter, the last soul holder.

The rest of the prisoners were an odd mixture. From two female elves, to five male, pig-faced goblins, it was a strange assortment, seeing as most of the people in the cage were natural enemies...kind of like putting twenty cats in a room with twenty dogs. But they had worked together marvelously, evidently, since no one, at least that Cassandra could see, had been killed in that cage...at least not yet.

Cassandra couldn't stand seeing such a tormented group of magical creatures from her own realm. It sickened her to the point of nausea, and she nearly fainted into Caitlin, who stood still, white as stone, behind her.

Not able to stand it anymore, the young Air Fairy cried out and lunged forward. She didn't lunge forward with her hands, since there would have been no way she could have wrenched the bars apart with just her hands alone. But she stood in place and lunged forward with her magic. At first it was as if she were aiming for the prisoners themselves, and a few of them screamed in alarm as speeding cannonballs of wind sped toward their heads. Then the balls of wind shifted direction and slammed themselves at the cage door.

It ripped from its hinges with a loud crash, as easily as if it had been made of paper, and flew through the air, directly at Corner, who lithely moved out of the way. The iron door landed with a deafening crash at the stunned Caitlin's feet.

For a moment the prisoners stared, mouths agape, at the newcomers, paralyzed in utter shock. The first to move was Hunter, who shifted from a sitting position to a standing position as fast as his underweight body would allow him. Then he ran, or rather limped, to Corner.

When the boy was no longer behind bars, Cassandra noticed something about him that she hadn't seen before. A pair of emerald green, leaf-like wings sprouted from his back and reached toward the sky. They were small, not yet fully grown like Cassandra and Corner's, but they were beautiful nonetheless. Both wings curved outward and then came to a fine point where the top pair was closest to the sky; a thin strip of darker green decorated the middle.

Hunter was also wearing the standard attire of an Earth Fairy: a brown tunic, green leggings, both of which were slightly earth-worn. The sleeves of his tunic were cut off at the shoulder, and he had two short, brown ribbons tied to his right wrist. He didn't wear shoes. Most likely, those had been taken from him early on in his captivity. But if he had been wearing them, they would have been simple brown sandals, made of thick leather.

"You came!" he cried, his voice hoarse from lack of water.

Corner simply nodded, a small smile tilting his lips.

A tear fell from Emilia's eye at the heartbreaking sight, but she swept it away before it could fall.

Caitlin looked at Corner with new eyes, finally believing he was on their side—a friend...someone who could be trusted.

"Yes, like a good little servant, he did what he was told," a woman's voice said.

Caitlin gasped and pivoted swiftly. Emilia shuddered and moved closer to Corner. Cassandra's breath caught in her throat, and Corner moaned.

The Dark Queen, wearing a dress of black silk and a crown

of gold with onyx-colored gems, stood behind them. Her flame red hair was pulled back into an elegant bun. Stunning blue eyes glistened with brilliance as she watched the five soul holders with a smile.

Thirteen

They were trapped. No, not like stuck in a corner, I mean literally trapped in power-enforced boxes that Kendra had made from magic.

Almost as soon as the queen had spoken, her magic swept the room. Darkened glass, harder than any metal of this earth, sprouted from the wooden floorboards and separated the five soul holders, keeping them from completing the circle that would release Maddy's soul. Caitlin was trapped in a corner, closest to the prison at the end of the room. Cassandra's cell was located in front of hers. Corner was located to her left and Emilia was to the left of him. Hunter was in front of Corner, closest to Kendra.

All five new prisoners were surprised to find they could hear and see through the black glass making up their box cages.

"Good luck getting out of here. I won't worry about the old prisoner—" the door to the iron cage was still blown off—"since now that I have you, it really doesn't matter. Oh, and I think these two actors will watch over you nicely."

The two guards Corner had sent away entered the room as she spoke, grinning wickedly; obviously they had told Kendra about the intruders. Cassandra had to hand it to them; they weren't as dumb as they appeared.

"Don't let them escape." Queen Kendra chuckled. "Not that they can. They're mere children after all...but very *gifted* children nonetheless. So watch them carefully; don't fall for any of their tricks."

The guards bowed dutifully and took their previous

positions in the room, only this time they remained wide awake and on their guard.

Kendra, with one backward glance to make sure she had secured the soul holders properly, stalked out the door, pulling it shut behind her.

"So that's it, then," moaned Cassandra, leaning against the wall of her box and sinking to the ground. "We're done. After everything that's happened, we make one stupid mistake and it's all over."

"No! I refuse to believe this is how it's going to end." Caitlin threw herself against the side of her prison, trying to ram with her shoulder like she'd seen people in movies do. And, like those people in movies, all it ended up doing was giving her throbbing shoulder.

"Don't bother. These are reinforced plasma, a material men of this earth won't ever be able to dream of. It's even stronger then our fairy wings!" Corner murmured, his head pressed against the cool glass of his cell.

"But it's so... thin! I can see right through it. If it's so thin, then how can it be strong?" Emilia pondered, tapping the glass with her fingernail. It rippled strangely, like a hardened pool of water, under her touch.

"*Thin* may be the key word," mumbled Cassandra, low enough so that the guards couldn't hear her. She began tapping on the glass, trying to find any weak points, grinning at Caitlin as she did so, "Time to use that special power of yours. Remember what happened the night the shadows were attacking us? We grabbed hands and a white light appeared, part of Maddy's soul! It scared the shadows, and it may be intense enough to break through these barriers!"

Caitlin nodded, realizing what Cassandra wanted her to do, and took a deep, strong breath. The vampiress placed both hands on the wall of the box keeping her from reaching Cassandra. Immediately she began to sink in, and the guards began to shout in alarm, though they could do nothing. Each prison kept its captive inside, but those on the outside could not get through the strange, fairy material. So the soul holders were safe, as long as they stayed in their boxes.

The smooth, reinforced plasma bent under her hands, molding itself to her arms. It was like seeing Caitlin pull on a pair of dark, crystal gloves. Then the material started thinning and, after about thirty seconds, the tip of Caitlin's pinky broke free.

Cassandra then placed her pinky on her friend's.

BOOM!

It was the second strongest blast of white light they had ever experienced…second only to the blast they had experienced back in the prison of a hole on the mountain near Caitlin's hometown.

The guards, shrieking and covering their faces, in a desperate attempt to keep the light from hitting their skin, ran from the room as fast as they could, no doubt going to get their Queen. It was actually pretty funny, because on the way out the guards tripped and practically fell halfway down the tower's staircase.

Crash! Bang!

The walls of the boxes vanished as wave after wave of light hit them, sending most of their occupants flying in all directions. Corner was sent hurtling toward a sharp, spike-tipped object that wouldn't have looked out of place in some deranged horror film. He would have been stabbed through the heart and killed, if not for the fact that his wings caught him in midair and placed him safely on the wooden floorboards.

Emilia, during her flight through the air, transformed herself into a housefly, just before hitting the iron bars of the prison, which still held its stunned occupants.

Last was Hunter, who wasn't nearly as lucky as the first two. He tumbled through the air and landed with a dull thud on his bottom on the floor.

Caitlin and Cassandra, on the other hand, hadn't moved an inch. They were holding each other's hand, kneeling on the floor, and bracing themselves against the energy leaving their bodies. Their eyes were shut tightly. This time they had prepared themselves for the bright, nearly blinding flash, and their brows were furrowed in intense concentration. Finally, after a minute, they let go, falling to the floor with two shallow thuds, their breath coming in small, strangled gasps as their lungs clawed for air.

After she caught her breath, Cassandra noticed that the prisoners, who looked bewildered, were still in their iron cage. In fact, they were still sitting in the same positions they had been in when the four soul holders had entered the room.

Hunter spoke. "Half of them lost the ability to speak after the brutal torture they endured. The screaming made them lose their voices. It was... horrible." He shivered with the memory. "They probably don't have the will or energy to move. That's what torture does to you. Your body spends all its time and energy trying to heal itself. There's no time or thought for anything else."

"We've got to get them out of here. Kendra will come back, and this could get ugly," Cassandra said. She drew in a breath, strengthening her magic as much as she could. When she exhaled and blew, the silver healing glitter she had used on Madore and herself rained down on the prisoners.

A couple of the prisoners shifted, as if unsure of what was happening, while others' lips moved in what was almost a smile. Their cuts and bruises slowly began to vanish, and soon there were none at all. The skin of the prisoners became like that of a newborn, smooth and unblemished.

One Elven man, who looked like he could have been related to Caitlin's adoptive father, croaked, "It all feels like a bad dream...."

"Can you move?" Cassandra urged, knowing they had little time before Kendra would walk up the staircase and destroy them all.

"Yes, but you may need us. Half of us have plenty of magic to spare. Besides, Kendra could walk up those stairs at any moment; I wouldn't enjoy walking into her when she's angry." The elf man shuddered at the thought.

"All right, stay then." Cassandra grimaced, "Just please, *please*, don't get in the way, and close your eyes."

Most of the prisoners nodded, while others just simply closed their eyes.

"Quick!" Corner whispered. "She's coming! Get into the circle, but don't complete it. For now, keep two hands from touching…until Kendra walks in. Then those two hands have to be immediately connected!"

As he spoke, Corner moved to position himself between Hunter and Emilia in the circle. He grabbed both of their hands, and when they were in the correct position, light began to emit itself from their bodies. This light wasn't like the light that had surrounded Caitlin and Cassandra the first time they had attempted the soul release charm. It was like the magic in the room could sense that all the soul holders were finally together, even though Cassandra and Caitlin weren't in place yet.

The light echoed the color of the soul piece each soul holder had. The light surrounding Corner was black. Emilia's light, which surrounded her body with such radiance that it almost put the other colors to shame, was an angelic yellow. Hunter's was a deep, forest green. Caitlin and Cassandra didn't yet have their colors, but when they joined the circle, careful not to touch each other's hands until Kendra entered the room, Cassandra began glowing a gentle silver/white color, and Caitlin glowed an aquamarine/sapphire blue, outshining them all by a long shot.

"Be prepared for when she enters!" Corner shouted.

Caitlin and Cassandra simply nodded and focused their eyes on the door.

BOOM!

Dark magic hit the door so hard that it was ripped cleanly from its hinges and hurtled forward towards where Hunter was standing. A rush of wind, coming from Cassandra's direction, stopped it from landing on the small boy and flung it safely to the side. Kendra stood in the door, glowering, holding the frame with both of her hands, as though her body was pulling her away from the scene unfolding, but her hands were keeping her there.

"Quick!" Corner and Kendra shrieked at the same time.

***

Why Kendra helped in her own demise is still not known to this day, but the theory of what happened is that the good of Kendra's heart finally began forcing back some of the curse upon her body, freeing her hands, which held her in place long enough for the children to free Maddy's soul.

Caitlin reached down and grabbed Cassandra's hand before the Air Fairy could even react to the sight of the dark queen. The bright, different colored lights that surrounded the soul holders began to blend into one dazzling white color, which seemed to emit, not from one of them alone, but from all of them. Inside their circle was another dark blob, just like the one that had appeared in front of Cassandra and Caitlin. This dark mass changed into flat, paperlike star. It was unlike the one that had appeared in front of the vampiress and Air Fairy, since it was made of shadow only in the middle. The five points of the star lit up one by one with the white light that now encased nearly the entire room.

Then, after the points of the star were all lit, they began to fold into the middle part of the star, creating a strange, white pentagon that radiated power from every angle. This pentagon then exploded with such a crash that it put any other noise the soul holders had ever heard to shame, causing their ears to ring for days afterward....

☙❧

During the explosion, the pentagon released a young man, hardly out of his teens, who looked exactly as Queen Kendra had remembered him. He stood where the pentagon had been, and his form was made out of the same white light that had made up the pentagon. You could only tell where his features were because, in some places, the light was dimmer than in others. Maddy hadn't changed much after he'd encased his soul within five others. He was still handsome and broad-shouldered.

He was still the Maddy that Kendra loved.

The young Dark Queen, with all traces of hatred, cruelty, and darkness wiped from her face, ran toward Maddy's waiting arms. As she ran, her golden crown with onyx-colored gems fell off and hit the floor, cracking one of the precious stones.

Maddy and Kendra stood there for a moment, hugging each other tightly, until it was time for Maddy's soul to pass onto the world beyond the living. He held onto Kendra for as long as he could, but slowly his soul began to vanish from view. Soon it wasn't there at all.

Kendra didn't cry. She just stood immobile, staring at the spot where Maddy—and then his soul—soul had been.

Then, suddenly, she fell backwards, and hit the floor hard. Her eyes stared forward, not seeing the world around her, for she was dead.

☙❧

Caitlin didn't have to look at Kendra to know she was dead. It was as if the vampiress knew what was going to happen as soon as she saw Kendra's golden crown begin to fall....

☙❧

In the end, it was Caitlin, the vampires, who defeated Kendra. She grabbed Cassandra's hand and completed the circle, freeing Maddy's soul.

At the time, Caitlin didn't realize what that one move meant. But Corner, Hunter, and Cassandra, all of whom were learned in the ways of fairy culture, did. Emilia looked on curiously.

Corner, who held the second-highest rank in the Dark Fairy kingdom, stepped forward and picked up the golden, onyx-gemmed crown. Cassandra walked up behind Caitlin, placed one hand on her shoulder, and urged her down to one knee. Caitlin bent obediently, her legs shaking violently as she began to understand what was happening...what her role would now be.

"The cracked gem that broke when the crown hit the floor will always be a symbol of who wore this before you. Though cursed, she was still quite a remarkable young woman." Cassandra gestured toward Kendra, who now lay dead on the floor. "Remember always that we were all brought together for a reason. And as you bear this burden—until the day you produce an heir—think on this moment, as we all will. You will now earn a pair of dark wings, and like an everyday fairy, you shall fly with us, high into the clouds. This has always been your destiny, because fairies fly from birth. However, for the first time, you'll now be flying with wings."

Caitlin nodded, and Corner stepped forward with the crown. He placed it gently on Caitlin's head, where it rested lightly on her dark blonde hair.

"Behold, Dark Queen Caitlin!"

As soon as Corner spoke, a pair of dark, shadow-like wings sprouted from the newly formed muscles at Caitlin's back and stretched themselves out magnificently toward the sky.

About the Author

CARAMARIE CHRISTY's love of books started at a young age. When she was five, her mother read her the first Harry Potter book. At age six, CaraMarie read to her mother the next book in the Potter series. When she was seven, CaraMarie declared she was going to be a writer.

Growing up in a small town in upstate New York, CaraMarie didn't have a lot of access to books she enjoyed, but upon moving to Virginia, she continually found her way into bookstores and libraries. Little pieces of her world, and everyone in her world, inspire her characters. "I wrote *Fairies Fly* because I've always felt, at heart, that fairies are real. We just don't realize they exist," says CaraMarie.

For more information:
www.oaktara.com